Table of Contents

Finding Love in Seagull Bay
Dedication
Copyright 3
Act 1 – Chapter One 5
Chapter two 16
Chapter three 25
Chapter four 37
Chapter five 52
Chapter six 63
Act 2 – Chapter seven 72
Chapter eight 80
Chapter nine 89
Chapter ten 98
Chapter eleven 108
Chapter twelve 118
Act 3 - Chapter thirteen 127
Chapter fourteen 137
Chapter fifteen 147
Chapter sixteen 156
Chapter seventeen 165
Chapter eighteen 174
A Paul Watters recipe 181
Next in Seagull Bay 183

Finding Love in Seagull Bay

by
Michelle Hill

Dedication

To all the guys at Cannock Chase Radio for helping me retrieve this
file when my laptop died.
Thank you guys

*

Copyright

Copyright © 2023 by Michelle Hill
All events, places, businesses and characters in this publication are
clearly fictitious and any resemblance to real persons, living or dead
will be purely coincidental. They are all a product of the author's imagination.

*

ISBN: 9798865220954

Seagull Bay residents of book 3

Marcus　Christine　Tom　Morgan

Francis　Georgina　Katherine　Pharis

Reverend Townsend　Mrs Calloway　Pippa　Oliver

Ned　Francesca　Tammy　Rosie

Act 1 – Chapter One

Christine stood by the glass window in her salon sipping a cup of tea and watching the holidaymakers pass by. They were unmistakable amongst the residents of Seagull Bay in their bright clothing, flip-flops, sunglasses and sun hats.

The women often carried large seagrass bags slung over their shoulders brimming with beach towels, sun cream and whatnot and had excited children skipping along beside them, swinging brightly coloured buckets and spades. Whilst the men wore shorts, and if they were with their family, they usually always got lumbered with a cool box, as well.

Christine smiled at them and sighed as she contemplated what might have been in her own life if only things had worked out differently. A family of her own was what she'd always wanted, but that life was never hers to claim. She would have loved to have been blessed with children—at least two or three, and had always imagined having two sons close together and then maybe a daughter a few years later who the older brothers would lovingly protect. But God had made her life's path so much different from the one she would have chosen for herself. She sighed again.

The smile fell from her face as she thought of her ex-husband and how he'd ruined the special bond they'd shared in the time they were married. Now all those memories were tainted.

When they'd tried for children and it hadn't happened, they'd naturally sought medical advice. But the answer they'd received had not been what they were expecting. Christine wasn't able to conceive children. The results were a dagger to her heart—to *both* of their hearts.

After a few months coming to terms with the devastating news, Christine had suggested they adopt, but her ex-husband Sam, had talked her out of it, saying they had each other, and *she* was his everything and all he would ever need, insisting they'd concentrate on making the most of their life together instead. And over for the next few years, they had. Christine had been his—and he had been hers—love doves, as they called each other.

She placed her mug down and flapped her hands in front of her eyes to stop the brimming tears from falling. She couldn't understand why she was getting so emotional. The marriage had ended eight years ago. She was over her ex-husband and the life they'd shared. A line had been drawn under that part of her life as soon as he'd moved away from Seagull Bay.

It was a hard decision after what had happened, but Christine had decided to stay in the bay and carry on as normal—well, as normal as she could after a divorce. She'd plastered a smile on her face whilst putting Sam's betrayal behind her and throwing herself into her business and the life she'd built in Seagull Bay—alone.

Breathing in deeply, Christine looked up at the blue sky, drawing in strength from God—the one reliable man in her life. She chuckled to herself. God might well be a woman for all she knew, but to her, he was always a constant source of masculine strength she could always rely on.

She turned her attention back to the families passing by. It would have been nice to have little grandchildren to spoil, but at least she'd been lucky enough to watch the local children from the community grow up. She'd always been content making a fuss of them when they'd come into the salon with a parent to get their hair cut, spoiling them with treats.

A flash of grey hair bobbed past the window pulling Christine out of her daze and she turned to the door to greet her first client of the day—her dear friend, Morgan. 'Good morning Morgan. It looks busy out there today.'

Morgan smiled brightly at Christine as she came into the shop, closing the door behind her. 'Morning Christine. I think it's the promise of wonderful weather. The report hinted it would reach the high twenties today. I think it has everyone heading for a suitable spot on the beach.' Morgan's maple cane tapped against the tiled floor as she made her way over to the washbasins.

Christine made a move for the kitchen. 'I'll make you a brew before I wash your hair, love.'

Morgan settled into the seat in front of a washbasin and sighed as she smiled and nodded her head. 'Oh, that would be grand, Christine. I've not stopped this morning. The hotel is fully booked and Pippa, Declan and I have been flat out cooking and serving full English breakfasts. I think everyone staying in the hotel must have wanted one today. It was only supposed to be Declan's and myself working a shift this morning, but we were so busy I had to ask Pippa to come in and help.'

Christine paused at the door to the backroom and looked back over her shoulder. 'How are Pippa and Oliver getting on with the pub since they took over the business from Brett? I thought they might have moved into the upstairs apartment when they bought the pub.' Christine wasn't a nosey gossip.

But she loved to keep up-to-date with the community. Her neighbours had become more than just her friends these past eight years. They were more like family.

Morgan shook her head. 'No-no. Oliver didn't want to uproot Brett and me. Plus, he couldn't bear to part with his family home either. So after he proposed to Pippa, she naturally moved in with him. They've recently updated the décor of the old place and Ginger and Jess love living in the house because they have the run of the little garden.'

Christine chuckled. 'Little is the optimum word to describe the gardens of Seagull Bay, Morgan.' She disappeared into the back room to put the kettle on whilst listening to Morgan's soft laugh as she agreed with the statement. The streets of Seagull Bay were hilly. The houses small. The gardens, even smaller. But the love the residents had for their small seaside town made up for its unconventional layout and homes.

As she made tea, Christine looked around at the room which had been a large storage room ever since she bought the salon. Tom, the local plumber whom she'd known for years, who was also a long-standing friend of Christine's, would soon be here to continue the work he'd started on its refurbishment.

Months ago, whilst styling Pippa's hair, Christine had mentioned how she was struggling financially with the erratic trade between seasons and she'd mentioned the storeroom in passing to Pippa, who then came up with the marvellous idea of renting out the backroom as a dog grooming business.

The idea made complete sense. Seagull Bay was a coastal town renowned for being dog friendly. Lots of local residents owned pets, as well as the holidaymakers who came to the bay specifically because they could bring their pets on holiday, too.

Since Pippa's suggestion, it had taken months for Christine to save up enough to hire someone to commence with the conversion, but she *had* managed it, and now it was finally days away from being completed.

Picking up the steaming mugs of tea, she made her way back into the main salon and placed them down in front of the mirror Morgan would soon be sitting in front of. 'I'll leave your tea here love, whilst I wash your hair. It's hot.'

'Thanks Christine.'

Taking a neatly folded robe from a freshly laundered pile, Christine opened it and walked over to Morgan who held her arms up ready to push through the sleeves, a routine they'd mastered over their years of friendship. She tied it behind Morgan's neck and placed a cutting collar around Morgan's shoulders and a towel on top of it. Turning on the water, she checked the temperature as it came out of the showerhead. 'Perfect. Sit back, love and I'll make a start.'

Morgan sat back, placing her neck in the dip in the wash basin fashioned for hair salons and looked up at Christine. 'Pippa tells me the dog grooming room is almost ready?'

Christine squirted shampoo onto Morgan's wet hair and worked up a lather. 'It is. Tom will be in shortly. I think he's connecting the plumbing to the wash stations today.'

'Ah, that feels lovely Christine—just like an Indian head massage,' Christine tittered. Morgan said the same thing every time she had her hair washed. 'It's all very exciting, Christine. Have you found someone to rent it yet?'

'No. But I've had a few inquiries and there's a woman coming in the day after tomorrow to view it.' She washed off the shampoo and then applied a little more for a second wash.

'Oh Christine, something's just occurred to me. Will the owners and their pets have to walk through the salon to get to the back room? I don't think that would meet health and hygiene standards.'

Christine gasped. 'I knew there was something else I needed to do. Thanks for reminding me, Morgan.' She shook her head. 'No, there's the side entrance. I need to get a new lock for the gate though, because I have the only key and the lock is rusting. The new owner and clients will need to access the dog grooming room that way. I'll pop to Old Po's later on. If whatever you want to buy is not in his shop, it isn't worth selling.'

Morgan chuckled. 'That's certainly true.'

Christine washed away the bubbles and applied a little conditioner, working it into Morgan's shoulder-length hair. A tinkle of the doorbell made her look up. A woman accompanying a young boy holding a bucket full of sand came into the salon. 'I'll be with you in a second. Take a seat my love.' The woman nodded and settled into the sofa underneath the window and was just in time to stop the young boy from tipping the bucket of sand upside down on the table in front of it. Her voice was high as she chastised him.

Christine smiled to herself and waited for the little boy to glance her way. 'If you sit nicely on the sofa for a little while longer, you can have a lollipop in a moment.' She looked at the young woman. 'That is, if it's okay with you. They are sugar free.' The woman nodded with a smile.

Washing off the conditioner, Christine patted Morgan's hair dry. 'Shall I sit up?' asked Morgan.

'Yes please love.' She placed a dry towel around Morgan's shoulders. 'You can come over to the styling chair now. I think your tea should be cool enough to drink by now as well.'

Morgan clutched her cane and got to her feet. She dipped her head in the direction of the young woman and boy and smiled. 'You can see to them if you like, Christine. I'm in no rush. I'll sip my tea and watch the world go by for a little while. I do love the view from your salon window.'

'Only if you're sure, Morgan?'

'Yes. You can always wet my hair again if it gets dry before you trim it.'

Christine nodded. 'Okay love, thanks.' She walked over to the woman with a bright smile. 'How can I help you today?'

'Is there any chance of getting my son's hair cut? I meant to pop to the barbers before we came here for our annual holiday, but you know what it's like, everything is always left to mothers to do .'

'Don't we know it?' said Morgan from behind.

Christine nodded in agreement and walked over to the glass jar on her small counter by the door, taking out a lollipop as she answered. 'Yes, I can give him a trim now. Did you need it washed first?'

The woman shook her head. 'No, we've just come from the beach and we'll be heading back there after this. It's just that his curls get so knotted when there's sand in them, and I don't fancy another battle when I bathe him later on.'

Christine walked over to the boy and leaned forward as she presented the boy with the lollipop. He appeared to be around five years old. 'Here you are little fella. You can have this for sitting so nicely while you wait for me, and if you can keep still while I trim your hair as well, I'll give you another lollipop before you leave. Would you like that?'

'Yes please,' he said, taking the lolly.

Christine straightened. 'You have such beautiful manners. Can you come and sit in this chair for me?'

'Go get in the chair, Thomas,' his mum directed.

Thomas quickly unwrapped his lolly and handed his mum the lolly's wrapper. He popped the lolly in his mouth and skipped over to the chair. Climbing up onto it, he twisted around until he was sitting down with his small arms on the armrests and his legs swinging. Christine pumped the foot pedal, lifting the seat a little higher. 'I didn't know you were *Superman*,' she grinned at Thomas as he rose and he giggled.

Ten minutes later, Thomas was being handed another lolly while his mum paid. 'Thank you so much. I've never known him to sit so still. I bet you spoil your grandchildren.'

Christine's smile faltered ever-so-slightly. 'Yes, I do... Please call again if you ever holiday here in the future. It would be lovely to see you both again.'

'We will.' The young woman waved her goodbye and pulled the door closed behind them.

Turning back to Morgan, Christine pulled her smile back into place. 'Thanks for that, Morgan. I would have had my own mini beach in here if little Thomas had been made to wait much longer.'

'No bother, Christine. Although I could do with another cuppa now before you make a start on my trim.'

'Of course. I'm a bit parched myself after entertaining Thomas. It was such a shame to cut off those lovely blond curls, but I can only imagine how knotted they would get after a day at the beach.'

'Yes. Marie used to have a job and a half with Pippa's hair when she was a nipper. She used to get me to brush it after she'd been playing in the sea because she knew I wouldn't be fazed by Pippa's crocodile tears.' Morgan huffed out a small laugh, her eyes glazing over as she reminisced. 'That girl had me wrapped around her little finger as soon as she was born.' Christine gazed lovingly at her friend before going into the backroom. Like Christine, Morgan had never had children, but after her husband had died young, Morgan had never remarried. Christine sighed to herself. Yes, God had a different plan for everyone.

The phone in the salon rang out as Christine stirred the mugs of tea. Picking them up, she carried them into the shop and placed them in front of Morgan before answering it. 'Christine's salon, how can I help you?'

Tom's dulcet tones were unmistakable on the other end of the line. 'Morning Christine. I'm so sorry, but I'm running late this morning. Can you believe it? Of all people, I bumped into Jenny this morning whilst I was in the city getting the fittings for the new dog grooming wash stations.'

Christine tried not to let her expelled sigh carry down the line to Tom's ears.

Tom had tried online dating six months ago, something that had taken everyone by surprise. It was the first time he'd considered dating since losing his wife more than twenty years ago, not long after their second daughter was born. At the time, it was an enormous shock to the community, the sad news devastating everyone. Tom had been a shell of himself for years, but he'd gone on to raise his daughters alone, successfully going it alone and shaping them into wonderful little girls. Now, they were lovely young women and a credit to him.

The single women of Seagull Bay had been quite put out when he'd made no attempt to pursue any one of them, even years after the tragedy. So when Tom had showed up at The Cheese Wedge and Pickles with a woman *not* from Seagull Bay hanging from his arm–someone he'd met online, there was a secret uproar between the spinsters of the bay and a fair few feathers ruffled as well. Tom was, after all, a handsome and hardworking man who'd raised his daughters single-handedly. He was the most sought-after bachelor of Seagull Bay. What was there not to like about him?

But the relationship ended abruptly when the woman called things off. Tom had been devastated, and he'd used Christine's shoulder to cry on. She'd done her best to support him for the last three months since the break-up, but it was starting to wear her down. It had taken time to shed all negativity from her life after her ex had walked out on her, and Tom's break-up had dredged up memories of that painful time in her own past.

However, she was torn. She still wanted to continue to be the good friend and lend him her ear, but after working alongside Tom while he did the fit-out of the new dog grooming parlour, she'd had enough of hearing him bemoaning about his ex.

Christine rolled her eyes. 'Oh dear. Well. It was bound to happen sooner than later, wasn't it Tom?'

'I'm still shaking Christine... Anyway, I'm on my way back to Seagull Bay now. I'll tell you all about it when I get there.' He ended the call and this time Christine moaned aloud.

'Oh no. That sounds ominous. Most unlike you, Christine.'

Christine turned to face Morgan. 'Sorry love. I hate to moan, but it's Tom. I love him to bits, but he's getting me down.'

Morgan's brow rose. 'Really? How come?'

'It's his break-up. He's still not over it, and muggins here is still his shoulder to cry on. Only, it's starting to get me down.'

Morgan frowned. 'But wasn't the break-up three months or so ago?'

'Yes, it was.'

'Crikey Christine. You must be a saint in disguise. You need to tell him you can't help him any longer, otherwise he'll end up dragging you down.'

Christine nodded in agreement, but her stomach knotted at the thought of the conversation of letting Tom know how she felt about it. 'I will Morgan...but I'll wait until he's finished working here in case he takes it badly.'

'I can have a word with him on your behalf if you prefer? I'll tell him politely you have enough on your plate with your new business and you can't have any negativity around you.'

Christine shook her head and grimaced. 'Thank you, Morgan, but no. I've been there for him since the start. I'll handle it.' When she found the optimal time to broach the subject, Christine really hoped she could find the right words. Her chest tightened at the prospect. She didn't want to upset Tom further, or worse, rock the foundations of their friendship.

Chapter two

Christine was sweeping up the hair from the salon floor when Tom came into the salon weighed down by the purchases he'd made in the city to finish the plumbing for the wash stations in the dog grooming room.

He smiled at her, but his lips were thin and the smile didn't reach his eyes. 'Morning Christine.'

She could see he was troubled and her gut tightened when she sensed his sadness. It was coming off him in waves. Seeing Jenny in the city must have really knocked him for six, but she didn't want to pander to him too much, otherwise he'd bend her ear at every opportunity today, wanting to talk through every second of the chance meeting with his ex.

Plastering a bright smile on her face, Christine decided to avoid mentioning the incident. Usually, she was always the one to enquire about how his day was going, and if he happened to bring up the subject of his ex, she always gave him time to talk things through. But that would start an avalanche of emotions. However, today she really didn't feel like getting buried under his feelings.

'Morning Tom.' She pointed to the parts. 'Are those the last items we need to finish?'

He nodded as he slowly made his way to the back room. Was it Christine's imagination, or was he giving her puppy eyes as he looked back at her in the hope she would ask about his well-being?

'Yes. If there are no mishaps, I should have it all wrapped up come closing time.' He paused by the door to the back room and looked at her. 'Shall I put the kettle on and make us a brew? Then I can tell you about Jenny whilst it's quiet.'

Christine's shoulders dropped. She nodded and forced a smile. 'Yes. That would be grand.' Looking outside her large salon window at the people walking by, she willed one of them to come in and save her. But it appeared no one was in need of a haircut—typical.

She sighed, feeling frustrated by the lack of custom. This was the reason she was making use of the backroom and letting it out. There was no consistency anymore. At one time, summer and high season in the bay guaranteed non-stop trade. Not anymore. That was why she'd had to think outside of the box of another way to bring revenue her way. Soon, at least she'd have rent money from the dog grooming parlour to fall back on in hard times, and she even hoped there might be a transition between trades. Hopefully, she'd get clients from the dog grooming parlour, and maybe clients from the salon would take their pets there.

Depositing the swept up hair into the bin, she heard the tinkle of a spoon stirring inside a mug. Tea was made. With a sigh, she put the pan and brush down, straightened her back, and headed for the back room.

Tom handed her a steaming mug as she walked in. 'Thanks Tom.' Distracted by her thoughts and not wanting to draw attention to the elephant in the room—that being the untimely meeting between Tom and his ex in the city. Subconsciously, she took a sip of her tea and burnt the edge of her lip. 'Ouch!'

Tom rushed forward. 'Are you alright Christine?'

Her fingers were by her mouth and delicately tapped on the scolded lip. 'Foolishly burnt myself. I should have known better.'

'Here.' Tom took her mug from her and placed it down. Grabbing a tea towel, he turned on the cold tap and held the edge of the towel underneath the flowing water before walking up to Christine and sliding his free hand around her waist to pull her closer to him. She squeaked in surprise until he cradled the wetted towel against her lip.

Christine's brow rose. She'd never been this close physically to Tom before. Other than the odd hair cut here and there for the occasional male customer, she'd never been this close to a man since her divorce. Tom's grip was strong yet tender. He felt so…so, *masculine*. Christine felt her cheeks heat. Tom was a very-very handsome man, and quite a few of her single friends had yearned for him from afar for years, but she'd never seen him in *that* light before. He was her friend—to her he was just Tom the plumber. But being held in a man's embrace again after eight years was stirring feelings in Christine she thought she had buried for good.

She shook herself free and took hold of the tea towel, accidentally grabbing part of Tom's hand in her rush to escape.

'Erm…thanks Tom. I got it.' His hands were so big. Why hadn't she noticed that about him before? Why would she?

'Are you sure you're alright?' He took a step towards her again and hooked his finger under her chin, upturning her face as he tried to examine her lip, which was an impossible task because of the tea towel blocking it.

To her astonishment, Christine's own examination of her *friend* continued. His lashes were so long and thick—his eyes were a soft blue-grey with a darker ring of blue around the irises.

'I'm fine—really.' She walked over to one of the seats she'd bought for the dog grooming shop still covered in plastic and sat down on it. She needed to get some distance between them and distract Tom from his concern for her. It was unsettling. Her heart was racing as if she were a giddy school girl again. 'Why don't you tell me about the incident in the city?'

Tom's demeanour changed instantly, as if someone had flicked a switch. He leaned back against the small sink and crossed his arms defensively across his large chest, whilst blowing out through puffed up cheeks.

He fixed Christine with a penetrating gaze that added speed to her already quickening heartbeat. 'It knocked me for six, Christine. I've been taking your advice and pushing Jenny from my thoughts every time she's entered my head. And lately, your advice worked. I didn't feel as sad when I thought of her and what could have been.' Christine nodded. 'But then, we literally bumped into each other as we each rounded a corner from opposite directions, and it was like, boom. A rush of emotions came back.'

Christine visualised the scenario in her mind's eye and after being so close to Tom, could actually imagine what it must have felt like. 'And? Who spoke first?' she asked.

Tom uncrossed his arms and his hands laced behind the back of his head as he looked up at the ceiling, his eyes fleeting from side-to-side as he remembered the meeting. 'It-it was me I think. I just kept on uttering her name, as if she were a spectre that had suddenly appeared before me.' He screwed up his eyes and his hands went to his face, covering it entirely before dragging down across his face, pulling his features down with them. 'I must have sounded so stupid.'

Christine shook her head and lowered the tea cloth. 'No. Not at all. It must have been the shock of seeing her, is all.' She was actually intrigued to know the outcome of the chance encounter now. 'What did Jenny say?'

'She said, hello Tom you look well. Sorry I can't stop for a catch-up, but I'm late for a meeting... Then she just disappeared, and I was left open-mouthed, watching her walk away.' Tom looked at Christine with a pained look in his eyes. 'I just let her walk away, Christine. It was the perfect opportunity to run after her and tell her how I was feeling...but I didn't.'

'Maybe it was the reality check you needed to make you realise things between you are truly over. After all, Jenny was the one who ended things between you. By text may I add. You never got proper closure—until today.' Christine really did hope it was the reality check Tom needed. Three months as his agony aunt was taking its toll on her.

'Maybe,' he shrugged.

His head tilted slightly as he narrowed his eyes and looked at her mouth. Christine suddenly felt very self-conscious. 'What's wrong? Is it hideous?'

The corners of Tom's mouth tugged up. 'No. Not hideous—I'd say—kissable.'

Christine laughed at his comment, dismissing it with a flick of her hand, but her stomach bowled over at its hidden innuendo. Tom's face was unreadable. Had he meant it jokingly? She couldn't tell.

'As long as I don't scare away my customers that's all that matters.' The door to the salon tinkled. Christine almost cheered with relief. She needed to get out of the backroom and away from Tom. She didn't know if it was a figment of her imagination, but she could swear the atmosphere in here had subtly changed. 'I'll let you get on with it, Tom.'

As she left the backroom, she was certain she could feel Tom's eyes following her every move.

A woman Christine guessed to be in her late thirties was standing in the centre of the salon, looking around the room. Christine greeted her with the same warm smile she gave to all her customers, even though the woman's critical examination as she cast sceptical eyes over everything hurt her feelings. 'Hello, are you Mrs Caldwell for a perm?'

The woman huffed. 'Goodness no. Perms were an eighties phenomenon. And one I hope doesn't make a return.' She shook her head and her long straight silky black ponytail swished like a glossy horse's tail. 'No. I'm here about the dog grooming rental. I saw the ad.'

Christine's brow lifted high. 'Oh...okay. Great.' She held her hand out politely. 'I'm Christine, the owner.'

The woman glanced at Christine's hand before planting a smile on her thin shiny red lips—a smile Christine noticed didn't reach her eyes. 'Hello Christine. I'm Anouska.'

Christine pointed over her shoulder. 'The grooming parlour is just this way if you'd like to take a look.'

Anouska scoffed. 'Are the clients expected to traipse through here with their pets to get to it?'

Christine's gut tightened as she shook her head. First impressions of Anouska were not great. 'No-no, of course not. There is a side entrance.'

'Ah. Good.'

Christine's smile was getting thinner by the minute. 'This way.' She turned around and led the way.

The door to the backroom was open and Tom was tinkering at the back. Christine stepped aside proudly to show Anouska the dog grooming parlour she'd invested so heavily in, putting her heart and soul into the project.

'Oh, no-no-no-no-no. The wash stations are in the wrong position.' Anouska shook her head and her hair swished from side-to-side. Christine's heart sank. 'They should be there and there,' she pointed. 'How am I supposed to interact with the help if they are left like that?'

Tom stood up and Christine could see by the deep rut between his brows he was ready to defend Christine's vision—and his work. 'But won't it be your job to wash dogs and not to worry about gossiping?' Christine cringed inside at his comment.

'I beg your pardon!' Anouska practically stumbled backward.

Christine raised her hands and fanned them up and down quickly diffusing the rising tension. 'I think what Tom is trying to say is, the way the stations are positioned now will enable you to commit your full attention to the dogs.'

Anouska shot her a quick glance. 'Well, I don't like them. They need their positioning changed.'

Christine's stomach dropped into her feet. She couldn't afford to get them moved. Her savings had disappeared after feeding the dog grooming project, and with how slow business had been lately in the salon, she needed to start earning rent from it to claw some of that money back, not spend more on it.

Christine hesitated before she answered, but she replied the best way she could. 'I'm really sorry Anouska, but with time constraints, it won't be possible to move the stations.' She didn't want to offer a reduced rental rate, but she saw no alternative. The ad went live as soon as Tom had commenced work, there had been a few inquiries, but Anouska had been the only one to show real interest in it. 'What if I reduce the rent by ten percent?'

Anouska's pinched features softened slightly, but Christine could see her brain ticking behind her dark eyes. 'Make it twenty percent and I'll take it.'

Christine gasped. Tom stepped forward. 'No Christi—'

Christine held her hand up to silence him. 'It's okay Tom. That's still just about workable for me.' She turned her attention back to Anouska. 'Okay, but that's only for the first six months. After that, the rent will return to the advertised amount.'

Anouska's mouth puckered, but to Christine's relief, she nodded. 'Fine. I suppose I'll have to make it work for me.' She turned on her heels and headed back to the salon. Christine glanced at Tom who gave her a weak smile before she followed. Back in the salon, Anouska turned to look at Christine. 'Can you get the contract drawn up today? I want to be in there next week.'

Christine nodded. 'Ye-yes. I can do that. How will I contact you?' She had no real idea what the business etiquette was for accepting a deal, so she hoped Anouska would prompt her.

'I'll call you soon. I must dash. I did have one more place to view today. It's on my way home, so I'll need to call and tell them I'm no longer interested.'

'Oh okay. I'll sort out the contract and wait for your call.' Anouska held her hand out and Christine shook it. 'Speak soon. I'm looking forward to working alongside you,' said Christine.

'Hmm. Goodbye.'

Anouska left the salon in a mini whirlwind and Christine was left open-mouthed.

'Are you sure about her, Christine?' Tom's voice from behind her made her jump with a start.

She turned around to face him. He was standing at the back of the salon with his hands resting on his hips. 'Yes, of course I am Tom. She's the only interested party I've had.' She sighed, 'And I almost lost her with your comment.'

'Sorry, Christine. I was only looking out for you, like you've looked out for me these past few months.'

'Thanks Tom, I appreciate it, but I've done okay these past eight years without the help from a man, so I think I can manage.'

Tom pursed his lips, as if he was trying to stop himself from replying. He nodded and dropped his head. 'I'd better get back to it then.'

Christine felt a pang of guilt for saying what she just had, but she was all *Tommed* out. She would be glad when she was no longer his agony aunt.

Chapter three

When she closed her front door behind her, it was a combination of the seagull squawks and the smell of the sea that drew Christine towards the beach for an early walk. The harsh screech of the gulls wasn't the most appealing noise, but Christine had always loved it. To her, it personified home.

The fresh salty breeze pulled at her hair as she slipped off her shoes and walked barefoot on the sand, digging her toes into the wet, velvety texture the closer she got to the sea. Thank goodness the salon wasn't too far away from the beach because she wouldn't be able to put her shoes on until she washed the sand from in between her toes.

The waves tumbled over each other, racing towards her, and then retreating at the last moment as she walked alongside the shore, reminiscing of her youth and the wonderful times she'd spent searching for the perfect shell each time she'd come to the beach. Her childhood bedroom had bulged at the seams with shells. It was only the fact that she'd had to move every single one each time she was made to polish her room that had made her obsessive hobby cease. At her mother's suggestion, she'd finally relented and filled a bucket with her treasures to return them to the beach for someone else to discover.

Her eyes scanned the beach now, her childhood habit never lost. She spotted the back of a brilliant white shell half-buried and pushed her big toe underneath it to dig it up to the surface, smiling with delight when she saw it wasn't broken. Retrieving it, she placed it on the palm of her hand and walked over to the waves. Then bending down, she held her hand in position and waited for a wave to wash over the shell and rid it of wet sand grains.

The cold water was a shock to both her ankles and her hand when it swished over them, and Christine gasped with surprise. It had been so long since she'd been in the sea she'd forgotten how extreme the temperature could be, even when the last few weeks had been in the high twenties.

'Christine?'

Christine would recognise the melodious tones of the voice behind her from anywhere. With a smile fixed on her mouth as she turned around to greet Reverend Townsend. 'Timothy. Good morning. Looks like you had the same idea as me—a lovely walk along the beach.'

Reverend Timothy Townsend's grin matched the twinkle in his eyes. 'Oh yes. I do love a good stroll on the sand first thing in the morning to help me plan my day ahead.' He looked down at Christine's polished toenails. 'But I daren't get my trotters out lest they scare anyone else away. Lovely colour, by the way.'

'Huh?' Christine followed his gaze and was suddenly self-conscious of the chosen pillar-box red nail varnish. She giggled. 'You are funny, Timothy. That's why I love your Sunday service so much.'

The Reverend chuckled along with her. 'And that's precisely what I'm doing now. I'm planning my Sunday sermon in my head. There's so much going on right now. So many changes are taking place in Seagull Baym, I'm spoilt for choice as to what to include.'

Christine reached out and squeezed his arm reassuringly. 'I'm sure you'll find the most important—you always do.' She breathed in deeply, enjoying the indistinguishable salty smell. 'Well, I'd better get going. I need to open up for my first appointment. I never know how Saturday's are going to be these days. I'm either run off my feet, or there's tumbleweed blowing across my salon floor.'

'Ah yes, of course. Hence the reason you opted to convert your backroom into a dog grooming parlour. You need to bring in more revenue. Have you found anyone to rent the room yet?'

She nodded, but without enthusiasm. 'Yes, although she isn't exactly the person who I'd envisioned to be my business neighbour.'

The Reverend's eyebrows lifted. 'Oh. How come?'

'Oh, don't get me wrong Timothy. She appears to be a lovely lady, but she bemoaned about the layout and asked me to move the wash stations. Of course, I couldn't do that. It would have hurt Tom's feelings to undo some of his hard work. He's as proud as punch with what he'd done so far. He's never done a complete refit before. The dog grooming parlour is his first one. Plus, it would have been an additional upfront cost, and I have no more savings left to raid. In the end, I had to offer it to her at a reduced rent so she would accept.'

The Reverend smiled serenely at Christine and the warmth from his smile reflected in his eyes. 'Ah well, the Lord does work in mysterious ways that we don't always understand at the time. I'm sure it will work out perfectly in the end, Christine.'

Christine wished she could agree, because there was a niggling feeling in the pit of her stomach which had started as soon as she'd agreed to rent the room to Anouska she couldn't shift. She forced her mouth to curl into a smile bigger than it wanted to offer at the suggestion. 'Yes, I'm sure it will. Oh well, I'd better be off. See you tomorrow Timothy.'

'Yes, see you at Sunday service, Christine. Bring your best singing voice.'

His comment this time made her laugh. 'I will.'

***

Katherine was standing in the middle of the shop with an enormous bunch of flowers. Her face lit up when she saw Christine. 'Hello my dear friend. These are for you.'

Christine's mouth dropped open. 'For me? Why?'

'For making my hair look so divine all these years.'

Christine took the bouquet and hugged her friend. 'It should be me giving you flowers. When are you leaving for your mums?'

'Tonight. I'm just packing the last of my things. Tammy, the young lady who's taking over the café is coming to my house later on to discuss the final details I need to pass on to her. So, this is the last chance to make my rounds and say my goodbyes to my nearest and dearest.'

Christine released Katherine and placed the flowers down to walk over to the washbasin and offer it to her with open hands. 'Then let me gift you a lovely new hairdo to send you on your way.'

Katherine chuckled. 'I wasn't planning on getting my hair done, but I won't say no to a freebie,' she chuckled.

Christine patted the seat in front of the washbasin. 'Come on, love. I'm going to miss styling those silvery locks of yours…

But I must admit, I'm going to miss your bacon butties even more.'

Katherine laughed out loud as she walked over to the seat and settled herself into it. 'Ah, get away with you.' She twisted around to look back at Christine. 'You will support Tammy won't you, Christine? Send customers her way? She's such a lovely girl, and I think she had a rough time of it before coming to Seagull Bay.'

Christine flapped a gown in front of Katherine for her to put on; an action practised thousands of times over the years. Katherine slid her arms into it and Christine swiftly tied it, adding a towel around Katherine's shoulders. 'Of course I will love. I'll even pass on best wishes on your behalf on my first visit there. How about that?'

Katherine leaned back in the chair, placing her head in the wash basin as she smiled up at Christine. 'Perfect.'

'How long do you think you'll be gone, Katherine? You are coming back to visit aren't you?'

'I really can't say how long I'll be living with mum, Christine. She's very elderly. She has all her faculties, but her body is letting her down. And yes...of course I'm coming back to visit. I've already decided I'm bringing mum back to have a high-tea at Tammy's Tearoom.' Katherine sighed. 'I really do hope it works out well for Tammy. She's decorated the place lovely. Wait until you see it, Christine.'

'I'm intrigued now, Katherine. Does this mean she's only selling tea and cakes though?'

'No, she's continuing to sell a lot of the hot food that was on my menu, but she's also adding her own spin on things. I dare say when I come back, I'll just retire and spend the odd day helping Tammy out.'

'Mmm, now that sounds like a plan, Katherine.' A comfortable silence settled over them as Christine finished washing Katherine's hair.

As Christine led Katherine over to a styling chair, a bang from the back room startled them both and Katherine jumped and clutched her hand to her heart. 'Oh my goodness. What is that?'

Tom appeared with a grimace. 'Sorry about that, ladies. I had to use the hammer to remove the sink. As well as being screwed to the wall, it was also stuck on by plaster.'

Tom's face lit up. 'Hello there Katherine. I thought I recognised those sultry tones. I should have guessed it was you.'

Katherine threw her head back as she laughed. 'It's no good charming my old bones Thomas Shelley, it's women like this beauty here who you should be complementing.'

Christine felt colour instantly rise from her chest right up her neck into her cheeks. She lifted her face but couldn't meet Tom's gaze.

'I think I've already ticked that box this morning, Katherine.' He pointed at Christine's face. 'Look at those for a voluptuous pair of lips.'

Katherine was now sitting in the styling chair and she stared in the mirror at Christine's reflection as she stood behind her. 'I knew there was something different about you. Have you had those lip filler injections I've seen some of the holidaymakers with?'

Christine flung her hand to her mouth, both in embarrassment and to stifle her laugh. 'Goodness no. I burnt my lips drinking tea just before you turned up.'

Kathrine chortled. 'Oh, that will be a funny story to tell mum when I get there.'

Christine dropped her hand and smiled at her friend. 'I'm glad I can entertain you.'

'Where do you want the sink re-positioning, Christine?' asked Tom. 'You'll have to share it with your prospective new renter as there isn't one in the back room now.'

'Oh, I hadn't thought of that, Tom.' Christine bit on her bottom lip in thought, and instantly regretted it. It was still tender. 'We'll need a communal place to make the tea and wash up won't we?'

Tom nodded. 'How about in your smaller storage room? It's positioned in between both rooms. All I'll need to do is plumb it in and send the drainage a different way outside. In fact, I actually have a pipe that will reach the drain.'

'Oh Tom, that's a great idea. There's plenty of room in there.' She furrowed her brow. 'Will it cost much more, though?'

Tom shook his head. 'Don't you worry. I've got other spare parts I can use as well.' He winked before he turned around and headed back into the backroom.

Katherine lowered her voice and leaned towards Christine as she pulled her mouth into a smile. 'Is there something I need to know before I leave, young lady?'

Christine lifted her eyebrows in surprise as she stared into the mirror at Katherine's reflection as she picked up her comb and began to comb Katherine's hair back. 'No, there isn't. Tom's just being Tom.'

Katherine chuckled. 'Is he now? I've never known him to wink at anyone before.'

Christine shook her head with a smile. 'What are you like Katherine?' But the seed had been planted. Was there more to Tom's actions and words today? Or was she reading too much into it? At least he hadn't gone on and on about Jenny like he usually did.

When Katherine and Tom had gone, Christine sat down in one of the styling chairs and watched the world go by. It was wonderful to have peace and quiet again now Tom was more or less finished in the new grooming parlour. There was no more banging and drilling. No more, '*Could I have a quick word Christine about Jenny.*' She sighed deeply. She hadn't realised just how quiet the salon had been before Tom had come to work in the backroom. She huffed with a smile. Was she actually missing his presence?

The phone rang. 'At last. A client I hope. I thought for a moment it was going to be one of those quiet weeks,' she said aloud to herself. Getting off the chair, she walked over to the counter and answered the salon phone. 'Hello, Christine's, how can I help you?'

'It's Anouska. I just wanted to let you know I won't be renting your dog grooming room after all. I found another rental that meets my needs much better.'

Christine's mouth dropped open. 'What? You don't want it now?' She didn't like Anouska very much going by first impressions, but she would have made their business relationship work. Now she hadn't a clue what she was going to do. Her mortgage was due, as well as her business rates. She would be lucky if she could scrape the money together to cover them after using almost every spare penny of her savings to get the grooming parlour finished. Then, where would that leave her for grocery money?

Should she try to lure Anouska back with another five percent drop in rates? She opened her mouth to do so, but her gut instinct made her hesitate. If she did, she'd barely be in the black at the end of each week. 'Okay. Thanks for letting me know.' She ended the call abruptly without the usual niceties and sighed. 'Odd decision, Christine. I hope you know what you're doing.'

Families filed past her window full of smiles. How had things turned on their axis again? The grooming parlour was supposed to be the answer to her money worries, but Christine felt as vulnerable as she had eight years ago, when she'd found out about Sam's betrayal.

Tears brimmed on her lower lids. She grabbed a tissue and raced over to the mirror to catch them before they fell down her cheeks, dragging spidery black mascara tracks in their wake.

The tinkle of the door signalled someone walking in and Christine sucked in a jittery sob that was fighting its way up her chest and spun around to greet the prospective customer with a fake, but very bright smile.

Her breath caught in her throat when a silver fox around her own age poked his head into the shop. His eyes crinkled at the edges and his brown eyes twinkled when he smiled at her with a toothy wide grin. 'Have I got the right place?'

'If you're looking to get those silvery locks trimmed, then yes.'

His musical laugh was just the tonic Christine needed. He stepped into the salon and Christine got her first glimpse of the body attached to the head. Dressed casually in a crisp sky-blue shirt and blue jeans, teamed with tan brogues, the man looked as if he'd just stepped out of a brochure advertising, *Next for men*. Christine's heart did a little gallop. As he took a step further into the salon, his cologne made her heart beat a little faster. Christine was a sucker for a nice smell, and when the nice smell came on a handsome silver fox, she didn't know if her legs would support her long enough to trim his hair.

'I'm actually trying to track down the owner who's renting out the dog grooming business. I have a cousin who lives here in Seagull Bay who told me about it.' His frown only added to his dashing looks. 'I do have the right place, don't I?'

Christine's head wobbled as she nodded far too long and for far too long. 'Yes-yes. The dog grooming rental is at the back of this shop.'

His frown melted away. 'Ah good.' A furrow quickly replaced it. 'Do you know if it's still for rent?'

'As a matter of fact, the lady who was due to rent it next week has had to let it go. Whoever is interested in renting it now is in luck.'

'Ah great. That would be me. Are you Christine, by any chance?'

Christine grinned. 'Guilty as charged.'

A well-manicured hand stretched her way—so different to Tom's calloused working-man hands. 'Marcus Mitchell.'

Christine slid her hand in his, glad she'd made an effort to paint both her finger and toenails. 'It's nice to meet you, Marcus. The grooming parlour has only just been finished. It's newly refurbished. It was an unused storeroom for years and a local resident came up with the genius idea to convert it. We are a dog-loving community you see, so whoever took on the parlour wouldn't be short for work.'

'When I was looking for a place to buy three years ago when I opened my first grooming business, I wished I'd listened to my cousin. But I was new to the industry back then and thought I'd do well to stay close to the city. But in hindsight, I could have started up anywhere. Pet owners don't care how far they have to travel as long as they receive quality care for their beloved pets.'

'Oh, so you already have a shop?'

Marcus grimaced. 'Yes, and no. I own a shop, but there's recently been a great deal of structural damage to it.'

'Oh no. What happened?'

'A lorry crashed into the front of the shop.' Christine gasped and her hand flew to her mouth. 'Thankfully, it was after closing time. So as you can see, I'm desperate to find somewhere fast because of my established clients. I really don't want to let down.'

Christine nodded in agreement. 'Yes, I can understand that. Why don't you come and have a look at the parlour, Marcus. Tell me if it fits your needs.' She crossed her fingers in front of her body as she led the way.

As they reached the door leading into the grooming parlour, Christine gestured for Marcus to go ahead. Marcus opened the door and Christine reached around the doorframe and switched on the lights. He stepped inside the room and stood motionless as he silently cast his eyes around the room. The seconds dragged into minutes. Christine's shoulders dropped. She had a feeling he was going to say exactly the same as Anouska had.

Markus's hands went to his hips and his head started to nod as he slowly turned to face her. His smile was back. Christine's stomach clenched with apprehension. 'It's just a tad smaller than the room I was using in my own shop, but other than that, it's perfect.' He pointed over to the other door. 'I noticed the side entrance outside. Does it lead to that door?'

Christine nodded enthusiastically. 'Yes, your clients and their pets have their own entrance. The only thing we have to share is the tea station.' She grimaced. 'I hope that's not a deal breaker?'

Marcus turned to look at her. 'If the rates are still the same as what you posted in the ad my cousin told me about, then no.' Marcus held his hand out. 'Is tomorrow okay to bring my stock in? I need to get some posters made up with my new business address so that I can advertise where my new premises are as soon as possible.'

Christine took his hand and shook it. 'Welcome to Seagull Bay.'

Chapter four

The temperature inside the church was nice and cool. Christine turned around on the pew to see who had managed to make this Sunday's sermon. She waved at Morgan and Brett sitting in their usual spot a few pews back. Old Po sat to Brett's right, but he was too busy looking around himself to see her.

There were all the usual faces attending the service, the residents who were around Christine's age and older. Paula and Phil, the owners of Poppy farm, were sitting at the end of a pew ready to make a dash back to the farm as soon as the service was over—their usual modus operandi. Christine applauded their stamina, they were always so busy.

Mrs Calloway, the woman who loved to keep abreast of Seagull Bay's goings-on, including what each and every resident were up to, including many of the returning holidaymakers, was talking quietly to Ned, the retired lifeboat rescuer. Christine grinned to herself. By the way he was crossing his arms, and had his mouth pulled into a thin line, he wasn't giving in to her questioning. He glanced periodically in Morgan's direction and Christine couldn't help but wonder if there was more to his glances than merely plain old curiosity.

The seat next to her was still empty, and she wondered how long it would be before it was filled again. Katherine usually sat with Christine, but she had left Seagull Bay last night for the long drive south, heading into the next chapter in her life to take care of her elderly mother. She sighed. She would really miss Katherine—and especially the bag of toffee all-sorts she brought along with her to every Sunday service.

The noise of the door opening and closing at the back of the chapel pulled her eyes in that direction, and she smiled, her heart swelling with happiness when she saw one of the younger families who lived at the edge of town had entered the church. They ushered in their two young children who were dressed in what Christine presumed to be their Sunday best. This was the first time she'd seen them here and she hoped they were the first of the many young families from the community to be drawn back to church to fill the empty pews.

The door opened again and Christine was bursting with curiosity to see which young family would enter next. But it wasn't a family. Familiar blue-grey eyes locked with hers, which widened with surprise when she realised who it was. Tom had come to church. Christine could count on one hand the amount of times she'd seen him in the Lord's house in all the years they'd lived in the bay—and one of those times had been to put his dearly departed wife to rest, and that had been over two decades ago.

Christine wanted to drag her eyes away from his, but it was as if they were stuck to him with invisible glue. It was Tom who broke eye-contact when he glanced at the empty pews the young family were settling into. He began to make his way over to them, but to Christine's amazement, he suddenly changed directions and walked her way.

In Christine's peripheral vision she could see Mrs Calloway had immediately stopped talking to Ned and her head was turning with Tom as he walked towards her. She could feel an enormous flush starting to spread across her chest, up her neck, heading straight for her cheeks. Mrs Calloway would have a field day if Tom decided to sit anywhere near her. Christine had already heard from some of the locals whose hair she'd done that week how Mrs Calloway had stated Tom had spent far longer working on her new dog grooming venture than he had on any other jobs in the bay.

At the time Christine had laughed at the absurd insinuation behind Mrs Calloway's remark, pleasantly joking with her clients Mrs Calloway was only keeping herself informed with the goings on in Seagull Bay. But now she was dreading what this might imply to Mrs Calloway.

Christine spun around to face forward again and watched Reverend Townsend make his way to the front of the altar ready to begin Sunday service.

The undistinguishable throat clearing of a male made Christine cast her eyes to the aisle. Tom was standing in it and leaning down close to her ear—his cologne entered her nose like a magical clear mist, elevating her heart rate.

'I-I thought I'd keep you company now that Katherine is no longer here.' Before Christine could answer, Tom was sitting down in Katherine's place.

'Good morning everyone. It's lovely to see you all again on this wonderful Sunday morning.' Reverend Townsend's melodic voice drew their heads forward. 'I'm absolutely ecstatic to see there are new members in the congregation.. My latest prayer has been answered. Let's begin by singing hymn number 106, *Just as I am*.'

Christine picked up her hymn book and subconsciously turned to the right page. The organ began and everyone got to their feet. Christine couldn't feel her legs as she stood up and how she was forming syllables to sing she didn't know. Her mind was still turning over the image of Tom in a tie, a crisp white shirt, suit jacket, and how devilishly handsome he was. Her stomach rolled over, and her chest fluttered. She thought her attraction to Tom earlier in the week had been a fluke feeling brought on by the nostalgic thoughts of the happier times with her ex-husband.

As he began singing, the hairs on the back of her neck stood up. How could a plumber who, as far as she was aware, belonged to no local choirs, have such a melodic voice? To say Christine was surprised was an understatement.

After the service, Christine naturally shuffled out of the church behind Tom, saying her goodbyes to the members of the congregation she had said goodbye to week in, week out for years. The Reverend, Timothy Townsend, stood at the door shaking hands and wishing his parishioners a good day. His face lit up when it was Tom's turn to walk past him. 'Ah. Thomas Shelley. Seeing you and the young family here today has filled my soul with hope. I'm going to make it my next mission to fill all the empty pews by the end of summer.'

Tom glanced over his shoulder in Christine's direction. 'I actually enjoyed it, Reverend.' He turned his attention back to the Reverend. 'I might even come again next week.'

'Our arms are always open and welcoming, Thomas.'

Christine watched Tom nod and move on, walking slowly behind people who were making their way back to the beach to retrace the steps they'd made to get here.

Christine drew her attention back to Timothy. 'Uplifting as always, Reverend. Thank you.'

'It was my pleasure. It was strange, though.'

He'd piqued her curiosity. Her eyebrows rose. 'Oh? What was strange?'

'Directing my sermon without the rustle of sweet papers to distract me.'

Christine's hand flew to her mouth to stifle her laugh. 'Oh no. How long have you known?'

The Reverend Townsend smiled serenely at Christine. 'Since the beginning. Since Katherine offered me one. Many-many years ago.'

'I feel awful.' She giggled. 'It's typical we get found out when Katherine's not here to take half of the blame.'

Timothy chuckled. 'Can I make a request?'

Christine nodded. 'Of course, Reverend.'

'Can I ask you to bring them in again next week? It wasn't quite the same not hearing them rustle today.' He glanced over his shoulder at a retreating Tom. 'Maybe you can share them with Thomas if he opts to sit next to you again—entice him to come back. Now that we have him here, we want to do everything we can to keep him, don't we?'

Christine nodded and smiled, though it was strained. She wasn't quite sure how she felt about the responsibility. Especially as her feelings towards Tom these past few days had been confusing. 'Of course Reverend. Right. Must dash. I've promised to help my new dog grooming tenant move his stock into the shop.'

Reverend Townsend clapped his hands together with joy. 'His? I'm sure you mentioned a female before. Have you found someone else to rent the parlour to?'

Christine nodded with enthusiasm. 'Yes. It happened really quickly after I was let down by the woman I mentioned. His name is Marcus. He needed to find somewhere fast for his established business and clients when his shop was damaged by a lorry. I believe he's opening tomorrow.'

'Wow. That's marvellous news. So we have two grand openings.'

Christine's brows drew together. 'How so?'

'Tammy's Tearoom opens tomorrow, and now Marcus's dog grooming parlour.'

'Oh yes. I completely forgot about that. I promised Katherine I would pop in and say hello. Thanks for reminding me, Reverend.'

'It's my pleasure. What's the name of the new dog grooming business?'

Christine grimaced. 'I honestly don't know, Reverend.'

'I'll just have to call in and find out for myself. It will give me a chance to introduce myself and maybe add a new sheep to my flock.' He winked at Christine.

Chrisitine chuckled. 'Be sure to come and say hello to me, too.' She walked on and then glanced back at the Reverend to wave. 'I'll make us a brew when you call in,' she shouted back.

The Reverend lifted a hand in a farewell gesture. 'Righto.'

Christine walked past the gravestones and then through the long grasses which led her out onto the beach. She gasped when she saw Tom was waiting for her, his hands stuffed into his pockets.

'I thought I'd wait for you so we could walk back together.'

'Oh right.'

They continued on in silence, side-by-side. The sun had already warmed up the upcoming day and she could see holidaymakers already basking in its warmth further down the beach. The sea was unusually calm and the only noise to break

FINDING LOVE IN SEAGULL BAY

the silence was the gentle crash of the waves and the squawking of seagulls on the cliff face not too far away.

Normally, Christine felt at ease in Tom's presence, but dressed so smartly and smelling so divine, it felt as if she didn't really know *this* Tom. She was so used to seeing the mucky overalls Tom. So when he started to talk about his ex again, instead of being irritated this time, she welcomed the distraction.

'She messaged me, Christine.'

Christine turned her head to see Tom staring at her profile. 'Who? Jenny?' He nodded. 'What did she have to say?' She could feel a small knot starting to form in her stomach, but she wasn't sure if it was from being over-protective of the man she'd grown especially close to these last few weeks—not wanting to see him get hurt again. Or because she was starting to get feelings for him herself.

'Oh, that she was sorry she wasn't able to stop to chat, and that I looked great... and that we should meet up for a drink.'

Christine grabbed the top of his arm to stop him. She was surprised by how big and hard his biceps was—why hadn't she noticed that before? 'You're not considering it are you, Tom? You've come a long way since your break-up. What if she's only being friendly, but you're reading it wrong and expecting more to come out of it? You'll end up back at square one again.'

Tom turned to face Christine. 'I know you have my best interests at heart Christine, but my heart was jump-started when I met Jenny after twenty years of...loneliness. Having a connection with someone—feeling wanted and wanting someone... I-I can't explain it.' His intense stare awoke something deep inside Christine. 'I *need* that in my life

Christine... Not one woman has shown any interest in me since Heather passed away all those years ago. What if Jenny is the only person who will ever see me as a potential romantic partner? I'm not exactly a young buck anymore.'

Christine spluttered an astonished laugh. 'Oh my goodness, Tom. Have you been walking around blindfolded all these years? Every woman who is single living in the bay, *and married ones come to think of it*, have drooled after you like a piece of candy locked away in a sealed glass jar made impenetrable by a magical spell for as long as I can remember... Don't you realise you are the most desirable widower in Seagull Bay?'

His eyebrows lifted slightly. '*Every* woman?'

Christine nodded with a smile. She couldn't believe his naïvety. All these years she'd thought he'd chosen to be alone. 'Yes. You could choose any woman from the bay—within limits of course. I don't condone going after someone who's married.' Painful memories came back to her in a jolt. They washed over her face and she couldn't hide them with one of her sunny smiles this time and she was certain Tom had noticed. She turned away and continued up the beach. 'I'm sorry, Tom. I need to get back. I have a lot to do today.'

He caught up with her in just a few strides. The silence stretched out between them, but it was the palpable tension Christine found unsettling. She could sense Tom wanted to talk more--ask her a question, but her tense shoulders and awkward movements were glowingly obvious she was done talking about his love life.

They passed the rowdy excitable chatter of the holidaymakers and climbed up the steps up to the beachfront,

Christine just in front of Tom. It was here they needed to go separate ways. Tom placed a hand on Christine's shoulder to stop her, and the heat from it seemed to penetrate her cardigan and seep into her skin. 'Thanks Christine. You don't realise how much you help me.'

Christine glanced back. 'It's what friends are for. See you tomorrow Tom.'

She walked away feeling awkward, knowing he'd be watching her. Thank goodness she'd decided to wear the wedges that weren't too high. She wanted to walk away looking glamorous, sophisticated and put-together. She hoped she didn't come across as frumpish and middle-aged instead. What was she thinking? Tom could have any woman. He didn't want her, and she didn't want him. He as her friend, and that's what she kept on telling herself all the way back to the salon.

But as she walked back, Christine played out their conversation again and again in her head. She was confused. Did Tom really want to be with Jenny because he loved her, or just because he wanted to be in a relationship? Was he only pursuing Jenny because he thought she was his only chance?

A voice pulled her from her thoughts just feet away from the salon. 'Good morning Christine. You look very beautiful today, but I don't think your heels and floral dress are appropriate clothing to help me lug my boxes of stock.'

Marcus's compliment flooded her cheeks with heat. 'Morning Marcus. She shook her head. 'No, I know. I have some work clothes in my salon. Two minutes and I'll join you.'

She couldn't get away fast enough to hide her crimson glow. But as she walked past Marcus's van, the image on the side and the name of his business instantly made her stop in her tracks and giggle. If he parked his van on the seafront, he wouldn't have to pay for advertising.

The name read:

Ruff to Regal Grooming

Christine carried on into the salon with a smile curling up the edges of her mouth.

Quickly changing into her work clothes in the storage cupboard with the newly plumbed shared tea station, Christine wandered through the adjoining door from her salon to Marcus's grooming parlour. She gasped at the pile of boxes neatly packed on top of each other against the far wall.

'Wow. You didn't hang about this morning, did you?'

Marcus placed the box he was carrying on the floor and straightened, putting his hands on his hips as he blew out through puffed up cheeks. 'I *have* to be open tomorrow. I have six regular clients booked in, and I'm expecting to get lots of interest from the local residents too.' He unfurled a poster, holding it up in front of Christine with the same cute puppy image she'd seen outside on the van. 'See. I even made the posters.'

'Oh yes. I remember I said I'd help you display them around the bay. The café has a noticeboard, but it's recently been taken over by someone new. I can go first thing tomorrow to see if it's still there. If it is, I'll pin one up for you. The noticeboard is very popular with the local residents.'

Marcus's smile made Christine's chest flutter. 'I'd really appreciate that. Thank you.'

'No worries. Now, what do you want me to do?'

'There are lots of small items in the back of the van that need to come in. They aren't heavy, but you'll be running backwards and forwards. I can make a start putting this lot where it needs to go while you get the last few things, if you don't mind.' His eyes swept over her, and Christine suddenly felt shy that her wide hips were no longer hidden by her dress, but were well and truly on display in her dungarees. 'Good job you ditched the heels.'

Christine laughed. 'Those were wedges. I stopped wearing high-heels a decade ago.'

***

Come lunchtime, Marcus's dog grooming stock was stored neatly alongside numerous bottles of shampoos, conditioners, hairspray canisters, perming and colouring solutions and whatnot in the storage cupboard, now also the tea room.

Marcus sunk into the elegant couch Christine had sourced from an end of line furniture store in the city for the parlour. He patted the seat next to him and Christine tentatively joined him, still a little in awe of his dashing good-looks. 'Crikey, that was thirsty work. Shall I put the kettle on?'

Marcus turned to look at her with a grin. 'How about instead I treat you to a drink and a spot of lunch in the local pub?'

Christine nodded with a smile. 'I'd like that.'

He patted her knee and Christine's heart sped up at the intimate contact. 'Come on then. You can introduce me to some of the locals.'

Christine studied his handsome face, the way the wrinkles gathered at the edges of his eyes when he smiled and the way he styled his tousled grey hair, which he wore swept back, gave him a distinguished look. Any single woman would be insane to turn down the offer of dining with such a handsome man.

Like a true gent, Markus held the door open for Christine as they entered the pub. She walked through the door and raised her hand in greeting, fixing a warm smile on her face for the few eyes that strayed her way. The locals who'd spotted her entrance waved back. But as soon as Marcus came in from behind her, stepping in front of her to lead her to the bar, those few eyes suddenly multiplied, as many more of the bay's residents' interests were piqued seeing their very single local hairdresser accompanied by a strange man.

At the bar, Marcus turned to her. 'What's your poison, Christine?'

Christine laughed at Marcus's humorous comment, drawing even more eyes their way. 'I'll just have half a lager, please.'

Oliver finished serving a customer and came over to them. 'Hello Christine. It's unusual to see you here on a Sunday.'

Hello Oliver. Well, we've worked up a thirst.' She gestured to Marcus. 'This is Marcus. He's renting the dog grooming room from me.' She looked from Oliver to Marcus. 'Marcus, this is Oliver, the new owner of The Cheese Wedge and Pickles.'

Marcus extended a hand, which Oliver shook. 'Nice to meet you, Oliver. So you've only just bought this place?'

Oliver nodded. 'Yes, I think we are just coming into our third month. My fiancé, Pippa and I bought the pub from Pippa's father.'

'Ah, that's nice, keeping it in the family.'

Oliver nodded with a content smile, obviously pleased by Marcus's comment. 'It is. I'm a very lucky man. When do you plan on opening Marcus? I'll spread the word to the dog-owning customers.'

'I appreciate that, Oliver. Thank you. Tomorrow.'

Oliver nodded. 'Consider it done. What can I get for you?'

'A pink and a half of Carling please.' PINT

While Oliver pulled their drinks, Christine felt a tap on her shoulder. She turned around to see Tom still wearing his Sunday best. 'Finish all your...jobs, did you?' He looked past her at Marcus, a sceptical frown furrowing his forehead as if he hadn't believed Christine's statement earlier in the day about having lots to do.

Her stomach knotted at his expression and his silent accusation. 'Yes, we got things sorted quicker than we thought we would.' Marcus handed Christine her drink.

'Who's your friend?' asked Tom, and Christine swore she could hear a jealous edge to his voice.

'Oh, I forgot to mention it to you earlier, I had a new enquiry to rent the grooming parlour. This is Marcus, the new renter.'

Tom's eyes quickly scanned Marcus from his head down and back up again, as if sizing him up. He transferred his drink from his right hand to his left and extended his hand. 'Tom Shelley. I'm the man who fitted out the dog grooming room.'

Marcus took Tom's hand and shook it enthusiastically. 'You've done a splendid job, Tom. It's exactly how I would have designed it.'

Christine waited on bated breath for Tom's reaction. A genuine smile split his face. 'Thank you, although I can't take credit for the design.' To Christine's amazement, Tom slid his arm around her waist, pulling her into him. 'My very talented and close friend Christine here has to claim the glory.' His grip on her felt more than overly-friendly. Christine was sure it was a gesture of possessiveness.

Feeling slightly uncomfortable in Tom's grip, Christine hadn't a clue how to shake herself free without making things...*awkward*. She laughed lightly. 'I think we can both claim the credit for it, Tom.' She pointed, drawing Tom's attention. 'Look, there's a free table over there, Marcus. Shall we make a grab for it?' She swiftly stepped out of Tom's arm. 'See you soon Tom.' Without waiting for his answer, she made a move toward the table. She could hear Marcus concluding their meeting behind her as she walked away. 'Come and pop in when you are passing Tom, see the wash stations up and running.'

'Thanks, I will.'

When she'd turned around to sit down, Tom was looking from Marcus to her, a perplexed look clouding his face. Guilt washed over her. She should have asked Tom to join them, but she didn't want to chance him bringing up Jenny and Marcus and her time being ruined by Tom explaining to Marcus about his brief online relationship that had broken his heart.

Was she being selfish? She pushed the thought from her head. No, she wasn't. She'd given Tom every spare minute she'd had these past six months, figuratively speaking, sparing him her shoulder to cry on. This afternoon, she wanted a conversation with a man who was full of hope—not despair. But the guilty knot in her stomach just pulled tighter as she talked to Marcus, because out of the corner of her eye, she was distracted by Tom's large bulk slumped at the bar, his head periodically looking their way.

Chapter five

Christine's chest fluttered with excitement as she walked to work. She held the poster Marcus had given her from his van yesterday evening when they'd left the pub close to her chest as she made her way to the new tearoom. Her tummy growled with hunger. She hoped to kill two birds with one stone. She wanted to wish Tammy, the new occupant well-wishes for the new tearoom from both Katherine and herself, and put the poster up there.

Today was also Marcus's grand opening, and she was excited for him. Yesterday at the pub, despite Tom keeping a secret tab on them, she'd had a wonderful evening dining with Marcus and getting to know a bit more about him. As well as being exceptionally easy on the eye, Marcus was amazing company too, and had surrendered story after story, keeping Christine in fits of giggles.

Katherine's old café, now a tearoom, looked amazing from the outside. The new sign made by Pharis after Reverend Townsend had called for offers of help in Sunday mass looked magnificent. The scrolled blue letters reminded her of art déco style and they looked amazing above the window lined with lace net and blue gingham curtains. On the sandwich board outside the tearoom, there was a wonderful picture of a teacup, and above it, a bundle of coloured balloons bobbed about in the warm breeze. The overall look was perfect for a grand-opening to greet her new customers. Christine smiled as she also noticed colourful bunting in the window as she entered.

A young woman who appeared to be in her mid-twenties with long brown hair scraped back into a ponytail was looking at a cabinet full with mouth-watering cakes turned around to greet her with a nervous smile and eyes as wide as a startled doe caught in headlights.

Christine gave her a dazzling smile as she approached the counter. 'Good morning Tammy my dear, and welcome to Seagull Bay. Katherine asked me to call in and show you a friendly face.' She extended her hand. 'I'm Christine. I own the local hair salon.'

Tammy was quick to take Christine's hand. 'Awww. How lovely of her. Hello Christine and thank you. I'm a bag of nerves and your wonderful smile is just what the doctor ordered. Can I get you anything? As you are my first ever customer, it's on the house.'

Christine was delighted by the warm welcome and sweet gesture, but she shook her head vehemently. 'Oh bless you, but I'll be paying my way. I want this venture to be successful for you.' She quickly scanned the new menu behind Tammy. 'Can I have a flat white espresso coffee and a toasted teacake to go, please? I have an early client and I'm not fully awake yet.' She laughed at herself, surprised she'd unloaded the personal information so easily onto Tammy. Maybe it was Tammy's large innocent eyes.

'Thank you.' Tammy smiled gratefully and stepped behind the counter. Christine watched her closely as she expertly set about making the coffee on the complicated coffee making machine Katherine had purchased for the café a few months ago. It never failed to impress her. Tammy glanced back. 'Do you take sugar, Christine?'

'No thank you. I'm sweet enough.' She giggled again. She didn't know what was up with herself. Was it the excitement of working alongside Marcus that had got her all a quiver today? She glanced around at the tearoom. Tammy had made a real effort to make it her own. She'd freshened up by painting and she'd hung new scenic prints on the walls. Up a corner, she'd added a small couch filled with colourful cushions, and a quaint circular coffee table in front of it. 'The place looks amazing, by the way. You've added your own charm.'

'Thank you. I wanted to add a touch more of the coastal town feel. You don't think I've gone overboard with the wooden whale figurines, do you?'

Christine looked at the little figures. Not doubting for a moment they wouldn't be a hit with young children. 'Not at all. They are my favourite part of the décor revamp.' She saw Tammy's shoulders drop as she sighed with relief. 'I notice you've kept the cork noticeboard. That's good because I wanted to ask you if I could pin up an A4 sized poster.'

Tammy gestured towards the corkboard. 'Of course. Pin away. I'm just nipping in the back kitchen to make your teacake.'

Christine walked over to the corkboard and moved a few cards to make room for the poster. The doorbell jingled and Christine turned around to see Pippa entering.

'Caught red-handed,' smiled Pippa, wagging her finger

Christine chuckled. 'Morning love. I was trying to make room for Marcus's dog grooming poster.'

'Ah yes. The handsome silver-fox you were seen out with in the pub yesterday. I've heard all about him. I'm considering booking in Ginger and Jess to get their claws clipped just so that I can be nosey.'

Pippa's first comment had ruffled Christine's feathers slightly. Had Tom been talking about Marcus and her after they'd left? She opened her mouth to ask, but the door jingled again and a holidaymaker came into the tearoom. Instead, she smiled at Pippa and walked over to the counter.

A moment later, Tammy came out carrying a paper bag. She placed it on the counter with her coffee and smiled at Pippa and the holidaymaker. 'Good morning.'

'Happy grand opening day,' said Pippa, making jazz hands.

Tammy chuckled. 'Thank you.'

Christine pulled her purse out from her bag and held it open, fingers poised above it. 'How much do I owe you, Tammy? And before you protest again. I'm paying.'

Tammy grinned and turned around, tapping buttons on the till. 'Four pounds fifty please, Christine.'

Christine selected the right amount and handed it to Tammy. 'Thank you, and I'll try and pop in later. But it all depends on how busy I'm going to be. The new pet grooming part of my shop is also having its grand opening today, so I'm hoping the pet's will bring their owners for a trim as well.' She laughed again as she walked to the door, suddenly nervous she'd be seeing Marcus again in a few minutes. 'Cheerio.'

Stepping out in the dazzling sunshine, Christine had a feeling it was going to be a splendid day. She passed a few holidaying families out early, strolling slowly past the shops, and pointing out displayed items in the windows, trying to entertain their young children strapped into buggies, until it was time to go to the beach.

The gulls squawked in the distance as they flew around their nests, positioned strategically amongst the crags of the cliff face, a familiar and comforting sound that had greeted Christine for decades in the bay. As she made her way to the salon, she looked out at the ocean and gasped. It looked quite lovely today. It had a deep emerald tone to it, and it sparkled in places where the sun's rays caught it, tricking whoever saw the magical flashes into thinking there might be hidden diamonds tumbling around beneath the surface of the waves.

As she approached the salon, she just caught the back end of a Dalmatian disappearing through the side entrance, leading to the door of Marcus's pet grooming parlour.

Someone else must have an early start too, she thought to herself.

Unlocking the door to her salon, she flicked on the light and then stood motionless as she listened to the muffled voices and dog barking coming from the backroom. This was the first time she'd heard the back room being used, and with the door closed, the low noise level wasn't too bad at all.

Christine smiled to herself as she turned on the radio and settled into a styling chair, placing her coffee and breakfast package down on the small shelf under the mirror to eat whilst watching the residents and holidaymakers of Seagull Bay stroll past her window. She had exactly ten minutes until her early morning client was due to arrive.

She was just putting her cup and paper-bag in the rubbish bin when the tinkle of the door alerted Christine her eight 'o' clock appointment had arrived.

'Good morning Mrs Calloway, you're right on time.'

'Good morning, Christine. I always keep my allotted times. Whether it's with the dentist, the doctors or even just to have my hair styled, I'm never late.' Christine smiled and shook her head as she turned away to grab a gown. Mrs Calloway was never slow in coming forward. 'I saw you helping the new pet-groomer to move his stock in yesterday.'

Christine stretched the smile she had plastered on her face a little further to stop herself from saying, *I bet you did*. Instead, she opted for, 'Yes, I offered my help because he needed to be up and running by today.'

'Oh...why's that?'

'Because his business is already an established one, and he needed to meet the needs of his current clients.'

Christine held the gown out for Mrs Calloway, who placed her handbag on the floor by one of the styling chairs before dutifully slipping it on. 'So if it's an established business, why did he move premises?'

Christine had known Mrs Calloway for a long time, she knew whatever you told her would soon be common knowledge to all residents of Seagull Bay and she didn't want to be the root for idle gossip, so she decided to act dumb. 'I didn't want to pry Mrs Calloway. Marcus was very busy and a little run off his feet getting the parlour ready.'

'Not too busy to take his new landlady to The Cheese Wedge and Pickles though, eh?' She lifted her eyebrows questioningly, as if expecting Christine to fill her in on her private lunch date with him.

Christine smiled serenely. 'All that lugging about gave us a healthy appetite, and you can't beat one of Declan's beef and Guinness pies now, can you?' Christine had to stop a chuckle escaping from her throat when she saw Mrs Calloway's face drop. 'How about a nice cup of tea before we get started? One sugar isn't it, if I remember correctly?' Mrs Calloway nodded. 'If you take a seat by the washbasin, I won't be long.' Christine turned away and let the triumphant grin pull up the corners of her mouth.

She was still grinning maniacally as she entered the storeroom where Tom had moved the sink into, along with the tea station. 'A little pussy and cream comes to mind.'

Christine was startled by Marcus who was standing by the small counter and stirring a spoon around a mug. She spluttered her answer. 'Sorry?'

'With that huge grin plastered across your face, you look like the cat who got the cream.'

'Ooooh.' She giggled, trying to fight off the mini volcanoes erupting underneath her cheeks.

'Come on, spill the beans! Has someone just proposed out there or something?' asked Marcus.

'What makes you think I'm not already married?'

Marcus shrugged, a boyish grin lighting up his face. 'Well, mainly the lack of a gold band on your ring finger... Unless you're allergic to gold, then that might explain the lack of a ring.'

A small smile played on Christine's lips. 'I was married once, but that's a story for another day.'

'So why the look of glee when you walked in here?'

'Well, that's because I thwarted Mrs Calloway's attempts at abstracting information out of me about you and your business.'

'Ah, I see. I used to have my own version of Mrs Calloway who came to my previous premises... Let's just say she was a good way of getting a twenty percent sale out and about without paying for advertising.'

Christine giggled. 'She's a lovely lady though, and keeps many of the older residents informed of what's going on in the bay. Anyway, how are things going so far today for you?'

Marcus nodded. 'Good. I have a steady stream of bookings from my old clients. I just need to drum up a bit more custom from hereabouts... On that note, I'd better get myself in there and introduce myself to this *Mrs Calloway*. I dare say word-of-mouth travels much faster and will give more clout than my posters ever could.'

Marcus picked up his mug of tea and tried to squeeze past Christine to get out of the storeroom, but even though it was a largish room, with Marcus's stock piled up in there as well as her own, in addition to the tea counter and small sink, it was a tight squeeze in there for two people and Christine found herself chest to chest with her new tenant.

She looked up into his handsome face and noticed his eyebrows were as immaculately maintained as his nails. The heat from earlier reignited in her cheeks. 'Erm, sorry. I should have gone out first.'

'No worries. If you just move your arm...'

Christine noticed her breathing had become a little more erratic. She couldn't remember the last time she was this close to a man. An image of Tom and her in here came into her head—strike that—yes she could. '...Like this?'

'There we go. Unstuck... Pop into my parlour when you find a spare ten minutes later on. You'll be able to see the grooming stations you designed working.'

Christine smiled brightly and found her eyelids suddenly had a life of their own as they fluttered for Marcus.

With Marcus gone, she quickly pulled herself together and made Mrs Calloway's tea, before heading back out to the salon. Mrs Calloway beamed at her as Christine placed her tea down beside her.

'I've just met you new tenant, Christine. Oo isn't he lovely? Sooo handsome as well.' Christine smiled, not wanting to agree for fear she might incriminate herself. 'And guess what?'

'What?'

'There's going to be a fifty percent discount on claw trimmings on Friday, but only for the first twenty people. Marcus told me he's not letting the sale be known until Friday morning in case he's inundated. I'm going to tell my closest friends so that they can be here early.' She chuckled to herself and Christine smiled knowingly.

After Mrs Calloway, there were another two appointments, but a free spell before lunch time, so Christine hung up her GONE TO LUNCH sign, locked the door, and headed for the grooming parlour. Standing outside the door, she could hear two muffled male voices. She hesitated with her hand on the door handle. Should she go on in, or knock first? She opted to knock to make Marcus aware she was there before opening the door.

To her amazement, Tom was there, cradling a small fluffy black and white dog. 'Tom? I didn't know you had a pet?'

FINDING LOVE IN SEAGULL BAY 61

His eyes swept over her, and Christine felt self-conscious all of a sudden. 'I've only just got her. She's a rescue dog'

Marcus fussed the little dog, bringing his face close to her snout. 'Yes, and I've now got lovely little Rosie here booked in three times a week for the next two weeks to make her all fluffy and regal.'

Christine felt a stir of unease. Tom had never once mentioned he wanted a dog. Was this a way of regularly coming in and seeing her? A free pass to talk even more about his ex? How much longer would he plague her with the dead relationship?

She forced a smile as she looked at Tom's little dog. 'Wow. She's lovely, but it's a big responsibility taking on a dog when you work full time, Tom.'

Tom shrugged. 'The circumstances are right for me... Besides, who could resist those big brown eyes?' Tom ruffled Rosie's fur and kissed the top of her head. She, in return, licked his face. Marcus and Tom laughed softly.

Ringing tones from inside Christine's salon cut through the laughter. She had been looking forward to spending time in Marcus's grooming parlour, but now she was glad of the excuse to leave. 'I'd better get that.' She turned her back to leave, but Tom halted her retreat.

'Have you got a spare half an hour sometime tomorrow to cut my hair, Christine?'

She'd forgotten she'd promised Tom free haircuts for agreeing to refit the backroom for her. Looking back over her shoulder, she said, 'Can you come half an hour before closing time?'

'Yes, great. See you tomorrow.'

Christine was already making up an excuse in her head of somewhere she needed to be as soon as the cut was finished. There was no way she planned on being Tom's personal agony aunt again tomorrow.

Chapter six

The next day started off much like the day before. Christine had the usual local clients, and then a lull in business. She stared out of the window at the passing crowds willing someone to bring in their children to brighten up her day so she could tell them silly jokes and make them giggle. There was nothing better to feed the floundering soul than the laughter of children.

Usually when the day was dragging, she'd pop to Katherine's café for a quick natter with her dear old friend. She'd only been gone for a couple of days, but Christine was already missing her.

Dragging herself away from the window, went in the back and stood motionless with her ear pressed against the door leading into Marcus's grooming parlour. Her brow lifted in astonishment. It sounded more like a party was being held there rather than a pet grooming business being conducted on the other side of the door.

Christine bit her lip. Should she go in and have a nosey? But before she could make up her mind, she heard someone on the other side of the door cough, and looked down to see the door handle moving. As quick as she could, she darted into the storage cupboard and grabbed the kettle.

'Christine!'

Marcus was calling her. She popped her head around the storeroom door. 'Yes?'

'Ah, there you are.' His toothy wide grin made her chest flutter. He looked even better-looking than she'd remembered.

'I have two clients here who wondered if you might be able to fit them in for a quick trim. They're men, but last night after hearing you agreeing to cut Tom's hair, I presumed you are a unisex salon.'

She nodded enthusiastically. 'Yes-yes. Send them through.'

Putting the kettle back, she smoothed down her hair and went back through to her salon. A moment later, identical men in their thirties walked in, their tight grins and darting eyes showing their apprehension.

One of them stepped forward. 'Are you sure you don't mind?'

Cristine shook her head and gave him her brightest smile. 'No, of course not. You can come through from Ruff to Regal anytime you are there for a trim. I'm open for business at the same time as Marcus.'

The other man sat down and sighed. 'Thank goodness. My brother is getting married in two days' time and as the best man, it was my job to organise not only for his dogs to be groomed, but for us to be groomed, too.'

The standing brother turned to face him. 'Yes, this idiot here thinks more about my pets than he does me.'

The sitting brother grinned manically and shrugged, his hands turning upwards. 'What can I say? They are prettier than you are.'

'Ha! You're mugging yourself off you fool. You look exactly like me.'

They both burst into fits of laughter and Christine looked from one to the other bemused. 'I bet you two were a right pair of rascals when you were young.'

The seated brother threw his head back as he laughed at Christine's comment. 'We still are.'

She walked over to a styling chair and gestured for the standing brother to come and sit in it. 'So where are you getting married?' She picked up a gown, holding it open for him to put on as he sat down.

'The Isle of White. That's where my fiancé lives. We can take my pets over there to be ring bearers.'

Picking up a neck collar, she placed it around his neck, making eye-contact with him in the mirror. 'Aww, that's so lovely.'

Christine chatted away to them as she cut their hair. She loved that she met new people and got to find out all about their lives. After they'd paid and gone back through to the pet grooming parlour, Christine considered her salon. Since she'd opened all those decades ago, apart from male children brought in by their mothers, she'd only ever cut and styled women's hair. There wasn't a barber shop in Seagull Bay and as far as she knew, men from the bay had to go into one of the other coastal towns or the city for a haircut. Had she been missing out on extra trade all these years?

She decided there and then she'd have a small plaque added to the sign above her door. The farm shop sold handmade wooden toys made by farmer Phil's son Pharis, and he'd made Tammy's new sign for her tearoom, so she wondered if he'd make her a sign, as well. She needed prospective clients to know she was becoming a unisex hair salon. She wondered if instead of having it say unisex, should she have the letters LGBTQIA+ put on the sign? She shook her head with a smile. How times had changed since she first opened the salon.

Come the end of the afternoon, Christine's bladder was bursting after making and drinking six cups of tea in quick succession in the hope of bumping into Marcus at the tea station, but they'd been passing ships in the night. But before she could run to relieve herself, the salon door opened and Tom walked in, his overalls pulled down and tied around his waist showing off his muscular arms and chest in his tight t-shirt.

Christine once again found herself appreciating his physique. For a man in his fifties, he would put many a man half his age to shame.

Tom studied her expression for a moment. 'You didn't forget did you Christine?'

Christine realised she was still staring at his rather large pectoral muscles and snapped out of her daze to shake her head. 'No-no. Come in Tom.'

As he turned his back on her to close the door, Christine quickly smoothed down her dress and patted her hair into place as she studied her reflection in the mirror opposite. She frowned slightly. Why was she making such a fuss? Tom was her dear friend.

'Shall I sit there?' he asked, pointing to the first styling chair.

Christine nodded. 'Yes, that's fine.'

He sunk into the chair and Christine stepped up behind him. Looking at his reflection, their eyes met. Christine noticed his lashes looked even longer and thicker from the angle she was standing.

Tom's grin had a boyish charm to it. 'I've never had my hair cut by a woman before. I usually go into the city.'

His admission confirmed what she suspected about the male residents of the bay. 'I can assure you, it's no different. Do you want it washed first?'

Tom shook his head. 'It's pointless. I'll jump in the shower as soon as I get home.' Christine nodded and reached for a robe. 'Don't bother with that either, Christine. These clothes will go into the washing machine tonight as well.'

Christine frowned. 'Are you sure? You'll get hairs stuck to your clothes?'

Tom nodded. 'Yup, they'll wash off.'

'Can I at least wet your hair a little to cut it?'

Tom nodded. 'Sure.'

Christine picked up a spray bottle and proceeded to wet Tom's hair. 'So, how's Rosie settling in?'

"Well, she stays with my eldest daughter, whilst I was at work, and then I collect her after I've showered. That was half the reason why I got her. Francis always wanted a puppy when she was young, but after Heather's passing, it was too much. What with looking after the girls and working. Now, she wants to get a puppy for little Francesca, but she wants to see how things go with a dog in the house before she commits.'

'A try before you buy sort of thing?' suggested Christine.

Tom laughed. 'Yes, something like that.'

Christine put down the spray bottle and picked up her scissors and comb. 'Just a shorter version of your style now?' she asked. Tom nodded. 'And what's the other half of the reason?'

'After having Jenny in my life for such a short time, I realise I need a female in my life.' Christine resisted the urge to roll her eyeballs. She wondered how long it would take for Tom to bring her up.

'I suppose you can't go wrong with a pet. There's no chance of them betraying or letting you down.' She was speaking from her own experience, but Tom naturally thought she was referring to Jenny.

'I wouldn't say she betrayed me, but I was definitely let down when she ended things between us... It-it was so out of the blue.'

Christine didn't respond. She didn't want to add fuel to this conversation. She needed to stamp on it—with both feet—from a great height. 'So what breed of dog does your daughter have in mind?'

'Oh...erm, nothing too big.' Christine began to cut Tom's hair. She could feel the heat of his gaze on her reflection, which was confirmed when she glanced at the mirror as she nodded her response. 'How's things with your new tenant? Do you see much of Marcus?'

There was an edge to Tom's voice and Christine couldn't quite put her finger on it. 'Great. Although I've barely seen him in two days. I've seen him once in the storeroom, and then when you were there when I popped in to say hello... Oh yes, and then earlier when he popped his head around the door to ask if I could accommodate two of his clients.' Christine glanced at Tom's reflection and she could see his jaw had jutted out slightly.

'No more romantic meals together at the pub together?'

Christine's response was a stuttered laugh. 'No...the meal we shared together on Sunday was a thank you from Marcus for helping him move his stock.' She expected him to respond, but there was a long drawn-out silence, which was unusual because Tom was normally as chatty as she was.

She moved in front of him and began cutting the front of his hair, but she suddenly felt exposed. She'd forgotten to put her overall back on when she'd gone to relieve herself, and with Tom also not wearing a robe, there was no formal barrier to separate them. This was another close and intimate experience—maybe even more so than on Sunday evening at The Cheese Wedge and Pickles when Tom had slipped his arm around her waist. That was an oddity in itself.

She could smell his personal aroma mixed in with traces of the same cologne he'd been wearing at the pub, and the combination made her tummy flutter. She listened to his steady deep breathing and wondered what it might be like to listen to that same steady breathing throughout the night. It had been so long since she'd lain next to a man, with her ear pressed against his chest, comforted by the strong rhythmic sound of his heartbeat.

Christine stopped cutting Ben's hair to take stock of her thoughts. What the heck was wrong with her? Tom was her friend—just a very close *friend*, she thought to herself.

'Is everything okay? You haven't taken off more than you need to or something have you?' Tom chuckled.

'Sorry Tom, I was lost in thought there for a moment. No-no it's fine. I've not scalped you, don't worry.'

'Thank goodness. I thought for a second I might have had to have it all graded down to a buzz cut, but I'm a little old in the tooth to carry off such a bold trim these days.'

'Hey, the word *old* is banned from this salon. I always say if you act and think young, you will always stay young at heart. How do you think I manage to stand for so long each day?'

Christine laughed lightly, glad to be distracted by her previous thoughts.

'I don't know about just thinking young. You look incredible, Christine. You have the figure of a woman half your age.' Christine paused what she was doing again, a little taken aback by Tom's frankness. 'I-I hope my comment doesn't offend you, Christine. I only wanted to compliment you.'

Christine drew in a long breath to calm her now elevated heartbeat. 'Erm, no... It's just that it came at me out of the blue, is all Tom.' She laughed lightly to try to brush over the now very awkward atmosphere Tom's comment had caused.

Markus appeared and Christine's tense shoulders dropped with relief. The timing of his appearance couldn't be more perfect. 'I've got a quiet half an hour, so I thought I'd come and see you in action, Christine.'

'Oh, there's no Indiana Jones action going on in here Marcus. I'm not sure this is the right place if you are looking to be entertained.'

Tom looked up at Christine as he spoke, his eyes dancing with mischief. 'There's no action, but definitely a little drama, Marcus.'

'Huh? What have I missed?'

Christine laughed nervously. 'Oh erm, nothing. Tom's just being daft.'

Tom turned to look at Marcus. 'We were talking about attitudes to age and I complimented Christine on her figure.'

Christine shuffled uncomfortably on the spot, wishing the floor would open up and swallow her whole to get her out of this awkward situation. She glanced from Tom to Marcus, willing her cheeks to stay cool.

Marcus's eyebrows shot up, as if he was as surprised by Tom's comment as Christine had been. 'Well, it's not my place to comment on my landlord's physicality, but for argument's sake, if she wasn't my landlord, I'd agree wholeheartedly with you, Tom.'

Christine gulped. She needed to nip this in the bud before she became a dithering wreck. 'Well thank you both for your input and let me return the compliment. You two are equally in good condition for your ages. I think we are all doing well keeping our engine's oiled and our bodies polished.' Thankfully, she'd finished Tom's hair. She put her scissors and comb down. 'How about I put the kettle on before I clean the hair from your shoulders?'

Tom stood up and brushed away the hairs from his shoulders. Not for me, thanks. I'd better get back. How much do I owe you, Christine?'

Christine flicked her hand away. 'Nothing. I said I'd cut your hair, remember?'

He winked at her. 'I actually did. I just wanted to see if you had.' Christine frowned. He looked over at Marcus. 'I'll see you tomorrow with Rosie.'

Marcus nodded with a smile. 'Yes, see you tomorrow.'

Christine watched him leave and then turned to face Marcus. His admission of her looking good had fanned the embers of her attraction for him—trouble was—she also had the same level of attraction for Tom. How had normality pivoted on its axis?

Act 2 – Chapter seven

Picking up her handbag from her dresser, Christine checked her reflection one more time before heading downstairs to Mina's Uber, waiting outside with Morgan already sitting inside, ready to drop them into the city for their monthly girly shopping trip and dining out day.

Picking up the post from the mat underneath the letterbox, she absentmindedly leafed through the letters, only to stop when she saw a letter addressed to a name that hadn't graced her doorstep for a very long time. It was a letter addressed to her ex-husband. Her stomached recoiled as memories of when she used to scoop up their mail and place it down in front of him at the kitchen table as he ate his soft-boiled egg and soldiers, a breakfast meal she lovingly made for him every morning before opening up the salon.

Why had a letter come to this address nearly a decade after their divorce? Would this mean she'd have to get in contact with him to pass the letter on? The thought made her nauseous. She turned the letter over in her hands, trying to find out if it was important or just junk mail, but there was no clue.

Tapping the edge of the letter on the palm of her hand, she was successful in dropping it down a few millimetres, and a few words appeared in the plastic window where the name and address were displayed.

She sighed with relief. It was just a sales letter from a company trying to sell house insurance. She threw the letter down on a side table. Later, when she got back from her day out, she'd write on it, return to the sender and repost it. Still, seeing his name again had rattled her. Lifting her chin high, she reached for the door handle. She wouldn't let it spoil her day with Morgan.

*

Looking out of the window of the high rise restaurant Christine placed her cutlery down and sighed. She reached for her wine-spritz and took a long drink.

Morgan looked up from her lunch. 'Oh dear. That doesn't sound very enthusiastic. Isn't your salmon en croute very nice this time?'

Christine placed her glass down and shook her head. 'No, it isn't the meal, Morgan. The food is as divine as it always is... No, it's my life.'

Morgan looked closely at her lifelong friend. 'What? *Your life*? What's wrong with your life? You are close to paying off your mortgage. You have a wonderful business, now with a side rental that will take the sting out of your bills. You live in the prettiest seaside town on the eastern coast of England...*and* you are healthy and beautiful. What's wrong with your life?'

'Well, when you put it like that, I shouldn't have any qualms with my life. Should I? And up until last week, I didn't... But something has shifted in me, Morgan. It started when I was watching the young families go past the salon window as I always do. I began to think about Sam, what he did to me and the children we could have adopted together.' She shook her head. 'I dunno. I suppose I'm just thinking of the, *what could have been*.' Christine looked deeply into Morgan's eyes, searching her friend's soul. 'Do you ever do that Morgan? Do you think about the life that should have been ours?'

Morgan sighed deeply and reached across the table, placing her hand on top of her friends. 'I do Christine. Every day. I wish I'd told Bren not to ride his motorbike that day...but...I didn't. I go back and forth between blaming myself and then resign to the fact that it was just his time and God's plan for him.'

Christine nodded sympathetically. 'I get that Morgan. I've said the same thing to myself about Sam. Maybe he was meant to have biological children. Maybe one of his grandchildren will go on to discover a cure for an illness or something. Maybe that's why God decided to make him stray and get another woman pregnant. Because I would never have been able to provide him with a child.'

'Who knows what's the reason behind God's plans.' Morgan squeezed her friend's hand.

Christine sat back in her chair. 'I've also been thinking, why didn't we ever date again, Morgan? We are both attractive women.'

Morgan looked thoughtful and turned her head to take in the view for a second, before looking back at Christine. 'I don't know. I contemplated dating again about fifteen years after Bren's passing, but then I second-doubted myself. I mean, who wants to date a disabled woman?'

'Lots of people. Your disability doesn't define who you are, Morgan. Geez. You are the most capable woman I know.'

Morgan huffed a small laugh, a smile pulled up at the corners of her mouth. 'Thank you. I appreciate you saying that. What's brought this on, anyway?' Her smile hitched higher. 'Is it by any chance that devastatingly handsome pet-groomer who I've heard so much about—your new tenant?'

Christine laughed. 'You don't miss a trick do you?'

'It's hard to, with Mrs Calloway living in the bay.'

Christine groaned. 'If I tell you something, will you promise not to judge me?'

'I'm your friend, Christine. I'll listen, make my own observations and judgement, and then I'll give you my honest opinion on whatever this is.'

Christine smiled warmly at her friend and nodded. 'I know.' She took a deep breath. 'For the last three months, Tom has bent my ear every time I've seen him about his failed online relationship.'

Morgan leaned forward, resting her elbows on the dining table, already intrigued. 'Oh yes. Jenny was her name wasn't it?' Christine nodded, 'And didn't she dump him just before they were about to embark on a three-week cruise or something?'

'Yes, she did.'

'That's awful isn't it? Especially as she was the first woman Tom had dated since his wife.'

'I know, but the awful thing is, I'm fed up hearing about it, Morgan.'

'Oh, I see. Well, in my opinion, your frustrations are justified. You've done splendidly as an agony aunt. Three months is a long time to lend someone an ear.'

Christine grimaced. 'Actually Morgan, that's not the issue I want to confide in you about.'

Morgan leaned forward even more. 'Really? Pray tell!'

Christine's head dropped back for a moment before she looked back at Morgan. 'I think I'm attracted to my tenant.'

Morgan shrugged with a smile. 'So what? From the descriptions I've had about him, I don't blame you.'

'And...'

Morgan's brow lifted into a sea of tiny lines. 'There's more?'

She nodded. '...I think I'm also attracted to—Tom.'

'Tom?! You *think*? You either are or you're not. So come on, which is it?'

Christine banged the heel of her hand down on the table with a wide grin. 'Darn it. I knew you wouldn't beat around the bush with your inquisition. Heads from the other diners turned their way. Christine giggled and leaned in closer to the table, dropping her voice. 'I do.' Morgan's smile stretched from ear to ear. 'But why do I, Morgan? I know a lot of the single women from the bay have looked at Tom in *that* way for years, but it's only recently happened for me.'

'I suppose it's like sprouts,' Morgan winked and then smiled.

Christine giggled. 'Sprouts? What do you mean?'

'You can dislike them tremendously for years and years, and then one day you look at them and think, I'll give you one more shot. You taste them, and then—*bam*—you're hooked.'

Christine wrinkled up her nose. 'I hate the smell of sprouts, but Tom smells divine.'

This time, it was Morgan who hit her heel on the table. Christine glanced at the other diners who were stealing looks their way again, but Morgan appeared impervious to the attention they were causing.

'I can't believe it. I've never noticed before, but you two are perfect for each other. Why didn't this happen years ago?'

Christine's brows drew together, forming a deep rut. 'Really? So what about my attraction towards Marcus?'

'Hmmm. I'm not sure what to say about that until I meet him, or at least until I see how the two of you react to one another... Hey. I have an idea. It's the bar-b-q at Poppy farm this weekend. Why don't you invite Marcus? That way, you can introduce me and I'll be able to secretly keep tabs on you both.'

Christine nibbled at her bottom lip as she thought about it. 'I suppose it couldn't hurt.'

'That's settled then. Come on, drink up. We've got some shopping to do. We need to find you a gown to wear to the ball, Cinderella.' Christine giggled.

For the remainder of the afternoon, Christine and Morgan went from boutique to boutique searching for the perfect dress for her. Finally, Christine spotted a rail of dresses that reminded her of classic 1950's swing-style dresses. She looked for her size and was ecstatic when the store had it. She held the white floral dress against her body to show Morgan. 'What do you think?'

'Oh my goodness. That's beautiful. Try it on!' Christine pointed to a rack of slim fitted 1950's style dresses with ruffled hems. 'Only if you try one of those on.'

Morgan looked to where Christine was pointing, and a small smile crept onto her lips. 'Do you think I could get away with it? It's a bit...revealing.'

'How can that be revealing? The sleeves come past the elbows and the hem falls way past your knees.'

'It will show off my hips.'

'And beautiful slim hips they are too. If mine weren't so big, I'd choose that style in a heartbeat.'

Morgan selected a mauve coloured dress and they headed for the fitting rooms. Ten minutes later, they emerged from their cubicles simultaneously and stared at each other with girly grins.

Morgan leaned on her walking stick as she appraised Christine from head to foot. 'Stunning, but you'll have to buy some shoes to go with it.'

Christine puffed out her cheeks. 'Have I come into an inheritance I didn't know about?' She smiled as her eyes skirted over Morgan. 'You need to wear dresses more often and stop hiding that fabulous figure of yours behind slacks and long-length blouses.'

Morgan turned around to look at her reflection in a full-length mirror at the end of the fitting room. 'I think you're right. I feel so free.'

'And you look stunning.'

'Are we purchasing?'

Christine nodded. 'We sure are, but then after we find shoes, that's it for me. I'll be no better off financially at this rate. I've already spent this week's rent money from Marcus.'

Morgan chuckled as she headed back into her dressing room. 'You can't take it with you, love. Can you remind me to pick up a new tie for Brett before we pay, as well?'

'Aww, you really do spoil your brother-in-law. I will... How is Brett doing? We don't see half as much of him as we used to when he was working in the pub.'

'Oh, believe me he still pulls pints every chance he gets. The reason you don't see much of him is because you rarely come to the pub on the weekend anymore.'

'I was there last Sunday with Marcus.'

Morgan chuckled. 'Oh, I know, and so does the entire community of Seagull Bay who like me, weren't there that evening. You know nothing stays secret in the bay.'

'Hey. I wasn't trying to keep Marcus's and my *work*ing dinner date a secret.' Christine smiled to herself and she walked back into the changing cubicle. She didn't mind wagging tongues speculating about the handsome Marcus or that they might be dating. It might drive more custom her way.

Chapter eight

Christine had overslept, and it seemed to have a chain effect on the rest of her morning. First she knocked over a neat line of shampoos in the storeroom that acted like a domino effect, pushing over the bottles of conditioner and toner. Next, her first customer of the day cancelled her appointment. And now she'd bumped into the table in front of the shop window where magazines with slick covers were stacked neatly for waiting customers to flick through. They slid off onto a pile on the floor, which was fine. It was the one magazine that had slid underneath the mini sofa that was the problem.

Christine got down on her hands and knees and then lowered further still to allow her arm to reach underneath the sofa to feel around for the magazine. Thank goodness she'd deep cleaned the salon last week and pulled out the sofa to sweep underneath it.

Just catching the edge of the magazine she pulled it out and blew off the few dust particles before pushing herself back onto her feet. When she pulled up into a standing position again, she all but jumped out of her skin when she saw a man's face squished up against the glass. The magazine flew to her chest as if it were a shield. It was the black and white dog in her arms she recognised first until the man's squished nose pulled away from the glass.

Christine dropped the magazine back onto the table and wagged her finger at Tom, mouthing, you gave me such a fright.

Tom gestured for her to come outside to him. She drew in a long breath to steady her nerves and smoothed down her hair before going to the door.

Tom greeted her with a sheepish smile as he petted Rosie in his arms. 'Sorry Christine, I couldn't see you and I didn't want to bring Rosie into the shop—health and safety you know?'

Christine nodded and found her arms crossing defensively in front of her chest. 'Not to worry...but, I really don't have time to lend you an ear to talk about Jenny today.'

Tom frowned. 'What?' Christine instantly felt guilt wash over her. Was she being harsh? 'No. That's not why I'm here. I have an appointment at Ruff to Regal for Rosie's first wash and grooming session. I wondered if you wanted to come and watch.'

Christine looked down at Rosie, whose large brown eyes watched her warily. She was such a pathetic little mite. Christine felt bad for not paying much attention to her before. Who knew what her life had been like before the dog pound.

She approached her slowly, and tentatively held the back of her hand under Rosie's nose for her to get a scent, then she gently tickled the back of her soft ears. 'Hello there, girl. Are you getting the special treatment today, eh?' Rosie's tail began to wag and Christine was glad she'd made the effort to stroke her. She looked up at Tom to find he was watching her intently. Christine's chest fluttered. 'Is your appointment now?'

Tom nodded. 'Yes, in five minutes.'

'Then I'm in luck. My first appointment was cancelled. I'll just make a brew and I'll join you in the grooming parlour.'

'One sugar for me, please.' Tom winked as he made a move to go over to the side entrance leading to Ruff to Regal.

Christine couldn't stop a smile from forming. Tom looked devilishly handsome when he winked at her like that. 'I remember.'

Minutes later she was kicking the bottom of the door to Marcus's grooming parlour with a mug of tea in either hand. Marcus opened the door and his eyes lit up when he saw the two mugs. 'Ah great. You must have read my mind. I'm gagging for a cuppa.'

Christine baulked and spluttered her answer. 'Sor-sorry Marcus. These teas are for Tom and me, but I'll make you one now.' She glanced over at Tom who had a smug grin on his face. 'I was just coming to watch Rosie get her first pampering.'

Marcus shook his head. 'Ah, don't worry. I'll make one after I've seen to Rosie.'

Christine's tummy pulled into a knot as she looked down at the teas. She felt awful now. She hoped Marcus didn't think she'd left him out purposely. Had Tom schemed the tea incident up on purpose? Christine shook away the idea. No. She was being silly.

Turning around, Marcus went over to a wash station and began to prepare it, selecting items from off the nest of storage trays nearby and setting the items down by the wash station. 'I'll be with you in a moment, Tom and Rosie.'

Christine walked over to Tom, offering him the tea, and took a seat next to him. Tom glanced at her before striking up a conversation with Marcus. 'Have you always done this for a living Marcus—groom pets?'

Markus shook his head. 'No. I was the manager of a sales company.'

Tom scoffed. 'That's like a teacher becoming a mud wrestler.' Christine glanced at Tom, unsure if his reaction was one to belittle Marcus. 'What did you sell—pet supplies?'

Marcus shook his head with a faint smile. 'No. Nuts and bolts for specialist equipment for the medical industry... I know. It's a world away from this,' he held his hands out to gesture to the room, 'but I got made redundant in lockdown. I needed a job I would look forward to doing every day. I used the money to start Ruff to Regal. The sales industry is cutthroat. I never want to go there again.'

'Can't be more cutthroat than plumbing, especially around here.' Christine wanted to roll her eyes at Tom. This wasn't a competition. Why was she irritated every time Marcus and him were together in her presence? 'There have been two large plumbing companies that have set up premises within a thirty-mile radius of Seagull Bay within the last three years alone. I can't compete with their prices. That's why I'm grateful for any work that comes my way.' Christine could feel his eyes studying her profile as he spoke.

Marcus took Rosie from Tom's arms, feeding her a treat as he spoke to her in a sing-song voice to put her at ease. 'Hello little Rosie. Are you here today to look even more beautiful?' He carried her over to a washing station, stroking her all the way. 'You are a good girl. Are you going to earn another treat by standing still?' He clipped a leash which was attached to the station onto her collar, all the while stroking her and talking to her in a calm and friendly voice. Christine was fascinated.

Marcus turned on the water and it spurted from the shower head startling Rosie. Tom was immediately on his feet, his tea sploshing over the edges as he swiftly set it down to stride over to Rosie. He brought his head close to hers and kissed her as he stroked her and whispered in her ear to help calm her down. 'It's okay my little princess. Daddy's here and I won't let anything hurt you.'

Marcus glanced over at Christine with an eyebrow raised and sent a silent message that Christine took as, *is this guy for real?* But Christine ignored it as she watched in fascination the love Tom was showing for the little dog, which had only been in his care for a few days. At that moment, she envisioned Tom rushing into his daughters' room in the dead of the night when they'd cried out in fear after a nightmare. No wonder he'd never bothered dating for all those years after his wife's passing. He was too busy being the perfect father.

For the next hour, Christine watched in awe as little Rosie, as good as gold, was carefully washed and groomed by Marcus under the watchful eye of Tom. She sat quietly and watched the two men as they interacted. Both were handsome in their own right. Markus was slick and well groomed, the perfect human example of what he wanted to portray to the owners of the pets he would care for. Whilst Tom was ruggedly handsome, the quintessential working man—all calloused hands and burly muscle.

Despite Christine's first impressions of Tom being in competition to impress her, trying to out-do Marcus any which way he could by making himself appear more knowledgeable about everything Marcus mentioned, she couldn't help but see him in a different light when she saw how caring he'd been towards Rosie.

After excusing herself, she slipped away back into her hair salon, ready for her next appointment, leaving them to fuss over Rosie as her fur was trimmed in places.

Sorting out the pile of magazines into a neater pile, Christine saw a head of dark hair walking past the window. She hurried out and called after the man it belonged to. 'Pharis!' He stopped in his tracks and turned around to face her. 'Christine. Hello. How are you?'

'I'm good. And yourself?'

'Busy. We have the summer bar-b-q coming up soon and I'm sure mum thinks she gave birth to an octopus. She's got me running around here, there and everywhere. I don't think she realises I have the shop to run on top of the toys, chutneys and whatnot I make for it. Are you coming to the bar-b-que?'

Christine nodded enthusiastically. 'Yes-yes. I wouldn't miss it for the world.'

Pharis' brow drew together. 'Is there something you wanted, Christine?'

She shook her head. 'Oh...it doesn't matter. I didn't realise you were so busy.'

Pharis took a step towards her. 'No, please tell me. I'm not *that* busy. I just go around telling everyone I am in case they relay the conversation back to mum. You know how quickly everyone gets to know everyone else's business around here.'

Christine laughed softly as she nodded her head and rolled her eyes. 'Oh, I know. You did Tammy's new shop sign didn't you?'

Pharis nodded, a proud smile lighting up his face. 'Yes, I did. Only took me a couple of hours as well.'

Christine pointed up at her own sign. 'I was wondering if you could make me a small plaque to add above the end of my sign telling potential customers I'm a unisex salon...I'm in no rush,' she quickly added.

'Of course I can. That's no problem. I'll make it the next time I'm in the woodshop making toys.'

'Awww, thanks Pharis. I really appreciate it.'

'No problem. You were the best hairdresser to ever trim my hair when I was a young boy. I hated having it cut in the city. I much preferred when mum brought me here and I got to have lollies and stickers for sitting still.'

Christine laughed. 'I'd forgotten about the stickers I used to give out.'

'Great childhood memories, that's what you gave kids from Seagull Bay who came to your salon, Christine.' Christine felt a lump form in her throat. It meant a lot to her to know she'd been a positive influence on the children in the bay. 'I'll drop it to you when it's done. Got to go. I'm heading to Tammy's to get lunch before I'm due back at the farm.'

Christine swallowed past the lump. 'Okay. Thanks Pharis.' She made a mental note to pop into Old Po's shop before closing time to see if he stocked stickers. He usually stocked all sorts of goodies.

*

Old Po's was like an Aladdin's cave. The only thing that had changed in the decades it had been open was the stock. The décor was still the same. The smell was still the same but best of all, Old Po himself hadn't appeared to have changed. He still wore the same style clothes he'd worn when Christine had first ventured into the shop. Heck, she wouldn't put it past Old Po to be wearing the *exact* same clothes.

She made her way over to where most of the stationary was [STATIONERY] kept and began to lift folders, and then notepads, only to put them down and search elsewhere.

A voice from behind her made her jump.' Looking for anything in particular?'

Christine spun around to find Old Po had crept up behind her with ninja stealth. 'Po. I never heard you walk up to me.'

He pointed down at his feet. He was wearing slippers. 'Touch of gout I think. Or arthritis, I don't rightly know. Blasted feet have been playing me up all week.'

'You should see the doctor,'

Po dismissed her comment with a puff from his mouth and the flick of his wrist. 'Pah. Doctors. How do you think I've survived this long?'

Christine smiled and shrugged. She had no idea, but she was eager to know the secret to his long life. No one knew his age, but according to some, he was at least at the end of his eighties or early nineties. 'Vitamins?'

'A drop of whiskey in my tea before bed each night and no sugar.'

Christine was more of a lager drinker herself, with an occasional white wine spritzer when she went shopping with Morgan, but she could easily slug a shot of whiskey each night. She envisioned chocolate eclairs and then a life without them. No, she couldn't do it. She would just have to go when it was her turn. There were too many sweet treats yet to explore. 'Ahhhh. Well, it's certainly working Po. You look fantastic.'

His chuckle was heartwarming. 'Flattery will get you everywhere, Now step aside and tell me what you're trying to find.'

Christine moved aside for Po to take her place. She had to stop herself from cooing at his petiteness. He was a little *Mr Magoo*—so cute. 'Stickers. I used to get them from here to give as rewards to children for sitting still when I cut their hair.'

Po lifted a pile of envelopes and nodded his head. 'Yes, I remember, But those ones were sold years ago.' He placed the envelopes down and reached behind a small pile of what appeared to be boxes of ink cartridges. His hand withdrew, holding two rolls of stickers. 'These are the only ones I have in at the moment.' He handed them to Christine.

She unravelled the first few on each roll to see what they were. 'Perfect!' One was a roll of cute kittens, and the other was a roll of cute puppies. 'I'll take them.'

Chapter nine

The seagulls were excitable as Christine made her way to Tammy's Tearoom and then she saw the reason why. Ben was throwing bits of fish from his cart onto the beach below the seafront. She waved at him and he waved back.

This morning, she'd decided to treat Marcus to a coffee and some treats for a mid-morning snack. She'd felt awful yesterday when she'd made tea only for Tom and herself, so this was her way of apologising.

The tearoom was busy. There were new Seagull Bay residents in there who she only knew to say hello to. The rest of the customers were holidaymakers. Standing at the back of the queue she waited patiently, people watching through Tammy's window whilst half-listening to conversations of the seated customers.

She contemplated her salon as watched and listened. Business had definitely picked up since Marcus had been there with at least one of his customers wandering through daily asking if she was free, and along with the rent she was receiving from him, financially, she could see a bright future.

Her life was nice. She worked at her salon five or six times a week, depending on the holiday season. She had a lovely home almost mortgage free. She lived in a picturesque coastal town. And she had a small group of friends who were fiercely loyal. So why was she feeling so unsatisfied lately?

A couple in their late fifties or early sixties wandered past the window hand in hand. Christine's stomach pinched when she remembered how Sam and she used to go walking each morning along the beach, hand-in-hand, just like the couple. Watching them, Christine realised it was the special connection with a partner she was missing. She missed the moments only two people in love could share and appreciate together—the intimate times and closeness only experienced with a soul mate.

At that moment, images of Marcus and Tom came to mind. They were the only men she'd ever viewed with romantic intention since she'd split with Sam. But why them? And why now?

Christine couldn't answer the question. Instead, she looked at the reasons why neither relationship would work. Marcus was her tenant, and Tom was her friend. It was as black and white as that.

Before she knew it, it was her turn to be served. 'Good morning Christine. It's good to see you again.'

'Good morning Tammy. I can see business is booming. Congratulations.'

Tammy beamed from ear to ear. 'Thank you, although I don't think I could have coped if I didn't have Declan helping me. He's in the kitchen preparing the hot food. I've been demoted to hot drinks and cakes.'

'He's a fantastic chef, so between the two of you, there's no way this place can fail.'

'Awww, thanks Christine. What can I get you today?'

'How about you make me a take-away bag of about eight different cakes and pastries? Oh, and I'll have two straight white coffees to go with no sugar, please.'

'Coming right up.'

FINDING LOVE IN SEAGULL BAY 91

Tammy worked swiftly, choosing sweet and savoury pastries with gripping prongs, arranging them carefully in a cardboard box, and making the coffees on the fandangled machine that made Christine's head hurt just watching her.

After paying and bidding Tammy farewell, she made her way back. As she suspected, Marcus's van was parked on the seafront not far from the salon. He started a little earlier than she did, so instead of going in through the front door, she chose the side entrance leading into Ruff to Regal.

With her hands full, she banged on the bottom of the door with her foot. Moments later, Marcus's face appeared with a little furrow in his bow. 'Ah. It's you Christine. For a moment, I thought I was in some sort of trouble with the police the way you kicked the door so hard.'

Christine laughed. 'Sorry. I guessed you'd recognise it was me because I usually do that from my side of the door when I bring you a cuppa. Anyway, I got you a coffee from Tammy's and some savoury and sweet delights in case you haven't had breakfast yet…but if you have, you can have them later.' She knew she was rambling, but she wasn't used to making sweet gestures for handsome men she may or may not be contemplating flirting with to get closer to them.

'What a lovely gesture—and a very welcome one at that. I overslept and then realised I'd run out of milk as well, but it was too late to buy some before coming to work.' Marcus stepped to the side and held the door wide to let Christine in. 'I've not long got here. I haven't even boiled the kettle yet.'

Christine stepped into the grooming parlour and placed the drinks down first before retrieving the box of tearoom delights from her own bag. She handed him a coffee and Marcus gestured for her to sit down.

'Thanks.' She looked around at the immaculately clean parlour that had been a wasted oversized storeroom and tearoom for years. Why hadn't she thought about utilising it much sooner? 'How are you settling in?'

Marcus gave her a dazzling smile. 'So much better than I'd dared hoped. The room is perfect, and driving into the bay everyday just lifts my soul. I don't know what it is. Whether it's seeing the sun shimmering on the ocean, inhaling the fresh salty air or the welcome from the gulls. I just can't wait to get here every day... I'm even contemplating a short-term house rental with a view to buying a house here at a later stage because I love it so much.'

Christine's mouth dropped open. 'Wow. The bay's really made a positive impression on you, hasn't it?'

'It's not just the bay. The local community and even the holidaymakers have made me feel so welcome.' Were Marcus's eyes twinkling, or was it Christine's imagination? 'And especially my landlady.' Christine could feel the heat release from the exploding capillaries beneath her cheeks as a blush tinged them crimson, but instead of trying to escape to hide it like she normally did, she embraced the natural phenomena. 'It's my pleasure.' Katherine's house suddenly sprung to mind. 'I know of a house that is up for rental. The décor might not quite be your cup of tea, but it's clean.'

'Really? Here in the bay?'

Christine nodded enthusiastically. 'Yes. My friend Katherine has a place here. She' recently had to move in with her elderly mother to take care of her and she's renting her house out for a short term, six-month lease, which she will review at the end of the term.'

'Do you have the agency number?'

'No, but it will be on the advertising board outside the house. I'll show you where it is after work if you like. It's just minutes away.'

'I appreciate that. Thanks Christine.'

'No problem.'

He grimaced. 'There is something I wanted to ask you, though.' Christine's stomach pinched, waiting for a complaint she hadn't seen coming. 'I know you have your lunch at twelve, but is there any chance I could ask a favour today?'

Her tense muscles relaxed as she nodded. 'Yes, of course.'

'It's a big ask and normally I'm fine, but today I think I'm going to need a second pair of hands.'

'I'm intrigued now. What is it?'

'I have a puppy coming in today and the owner has informed me it's a little nervous about water and she's having trouble bathing it. I wondered if you'd mind helping me.'

Christine's eyebrows lifted. 'Help bathing a puppy?' She nodded enthusiastically. 'Yes, I'd love to.'

'But it's a large puppy.'

Her head continued to bob up and down. 'I don't mind. I'll look forward to it.'

'Are you sure? I only need you to hold the shower head for me and move it to where I direct you.'

'Yes. I can do that. I've had a lot of practice,' she beamed before popping a small sweet pastry into her mouth whilst getting to her feet ready to go through to her salon and prepare for the first client.

Marcus sighed with relief. 'You're a lifesaver.' Christine nodded as she munched on the delicious pastry that was sending her taste buds into delectable ecstasy. She nodded again and held her hand up in a farewell gesture as she opened the door to her salon. 'See you at twelve?' Christine nodded.

*

When Marcus said puppy, he had actually meant a small horse somehow disguised as a dog.

Christine was wearing the oversized overall Marcus had given her, but as good as it was for keeping the splashes off her clothes, it did nothing to keep the water splashes from soaking her face and hair. As much as she tried to smile it off and stay glamorous as she was helping Marcus as he bathed the gigantic nine-month-old puppy, it just wasn't happening. The only saving grace was that the owner had dropped the puppy off and other than Marcus, there was no one there to see the hot mess she had become. All the extra effort she'd put into her hair and make-up for Marcus's benefit had gone clean out of the window this morning.

Had she really gone to that much effort to look good today just for Marcus? As she blinked away yet another blob of water flicked into her eye by the over-sized puppy, she realised she had.

The suds on the puppy were finally all washed off when Marcus released one hand from it for one moment to reach for a towel. One second was all it needed to start a full-length body shake, neither of them could stop. It started at the head and worked its way down its body towards its tail. Christine squealed as she laughed. Marcus apologised profusely through his laughter.

'Oh my goodness. I'm so sorry Christine.'

Consumed with fits of giggles, neither of them noticed Tom had entered the grooming parlour. 'I'm not interrupting anything am I?' Christine couldn't help but notice the annoyance edging his voice.

'Just give me one minute Tom whilst I see to this puppy.' He turned his attention back to Christine. 'I got this from here. Thank you so much, Christine. I'll take this not so little puppy over there to be dried. I'll come through and see you later on. Are you still okay with that thing after work?'

Christine nodded as she tried to smooth her hair back into some type of style again. 'Yes, of course.'

She watched with admiration as Marcus unclipped the puppy's collar and cajoled it to jump down and walk over to the drying area. When she turned back to face Tom, she realised he'd been watching her as she'd watched Marcus. The way he was looking at her now made her feel guilty. But what had she to be guilty about?

'Not opening up today? I tried your door and then noticed your sign was turned to closed.'

'Yes, I am. I was open earlier, and I have clients booked in this afternoon as well.'

'Oh right.' She noticed the cogs turning behind Tom's eyes. 'So your boyfriend couldn't manage the big dog on his own then?' Christine was mortified by Tom's comment. Her eyes widened, and she lifted her finger to her lips and made a shushing action to Tom. He ignored her. 'What? Is your relationship a secret?'

Christine quickly shook her head and glanced over at Marcus to see if he'd heard Tom's comment. 'No. We are not in a relationship. I am Marcus's landlady—period!' A look of relief settled on his face. 'Not that it's any of your business, anyway.'

Marcus strolled over before Tom could answer. 'Tom. What can I do for you?'

He glanced from Marcus to Christine and then back to Marcus again and Christine bit her lip, waiting on bated breath for his answer. 'Erm. Oh yes. I just called in to see if you'd come across a wrench since you've been here. I appear to be missing one.'

Christine's brows pulled together as she looked at Tom. She couldn't work out if that was the truth or not.

Marcus shook his head. 'No, sorry, pal. But if I do, I know who it belongs to.' Tom nodded. 'How's little Rosie doing?'

'Grand. She's settling in well between my daughter and I. It appears she has already gotten used to our shared caring duties.'

Marcus nodded with a smile. 'That's great. I'm seeing her again next week, aren't I?'

Christine shuffled from foot to foot, feeling a little awkward. A few days ago she was telling Morgan how much she was attracted to both of these men.

'Yup. Got to keep my little girl looking beautiful.' He turned to look at Christine and hovered a pointed finger a few inches from her face, swinging it from side to side as he spoke. 'You have a little...smudge, by the way.'

Feeling very self-conscious all of a sudden, her hands flew to her cheeks. 'Do I?' She backed away towards the door to her salon. 'I need to get back, anyway.' Feeling behind her, she reached for the handle.

Marcus grinned at her. 'Thanks for your help, Christine, and I'll see you later.'

Christine noticed Tom frown at his comment before she left. Her heart thundered wildly in her chest as she closed the door behind her. Placing her back against it, she breathed a sigh of relief. It was no good. She needed to speak to Morgan again. She needed more advice about her dilemma.

Walking into her salon, she headed for the nearest mirror to see what *the smudge* was, Tom had mentioned. She always liked to look her best and the thought of looking dishevelled appalled her.

But she almost fainted when she saw her reflection. Black streaks smeared both of her cheeks from mascara that was most definitely *not* waterproof, and her hair resembled an old bird's nest. Her jaw hit the floor. Even if she liked to think she might have been in with a chance of dating either Tom or Marcus before, after today, she wasn't so sure anymore.

Chapter ten

Peering in the window of Tammy's Tearoom, Christine noticed Morgan was sitting at a table with Ned the retired lifeboat rescuer. Morgan spotted her and waved. Christine waved back and then made her way to the door.

The smell of Tammy's home-baked cakes was enough to make the fullest tummy rubble and find room for the sugary delights, and combined with the exotic aroma of freshly made coffee, Christine was salivating before she'd taken two steps past the threshold.

Walking up to the table, Christine hugged Morgan. 'Good morning, love. You look beautiful.'

'She does indeed,' Ned agreed.

'I don't know what you two want, but keep those compliments coming and I'll gladly hand over whatever is it you are trying to get out of me,' Morgan grinned.

Christine laughed as she pulled away, smiling. She turned to look at Ned. 'Morning Ned. Are you joining us?'

'If I'd known you beauties were dining in here today, I would have taken a later breakfast and rearranged my plans for today, but I can't turn down the offer to do an off duty patrol with a couple of the lads.'

Morgan's brow lifted. 'You're going on a lifeboat now? After a full English breakfast? Won't you get sea-sick?'

Ned threw his head back and chuckled. 'Morgan. The lifeboat rescue crew don't do sea-sickness.'

She smiled serenely. 'Don't you mean *retired* lifeboat rescuers?' She wagged a finger. 'Just be careful.'

Christine nodded in agreement. 'Yes. Keep safe Ned. It's a beautiful start to the day, but I checked the forecast, and there's a chance of rain.'

Ned got up and tipped his cap to them. 'Don't you lovely ladies worry your pretty little heads over me. I've weathered storms many times, and there are no storms on the horizon today.'

'Are you coming into the pub for a pint of Guinness later, Ned?' asked Morgan.

'Do pigs fly?'

'No,' she chuckled.

He smiled, 'Then why ask such a silly question?'

Morgan flapped her hand at him, gesturing for him to go. 'Get off with you, ya cheeky beggar!'

Christine chuckled as she shook her head and waved goodbye at Ned. 'What are you having to eat, Morgan?'

'Scrambled eggs on white toast please Christine, and can I get another cup of tea as well?'

'Oo, that sounds good. I'll have the same. Okay, I'll just put our orders in.'

The tearoom was busy, but not packed to the rafters, but it was still early as Christine had wanted to speak to Morgan before she went into work today. Especially after what happened yesterday, and then after work as well. She cringed as she tried to forget all of yesterday's horrifying incidents. After her evening bath, she couldn't get to get fast enough to put a strike through the day.

'Good morning Christine,' beamed Tammy, 'what can I get you?'

"Morning, love. Two orders of scrambled eggs on white toast and two cups of tea with milk, but no sugar. You look perky today.'

Tammy sighed contentedly. 'I'm really happy Christine. I love it here. I love my customers and this little tearoom, but best of all, I can't believe how lucky I am to have my Uncle Ben.'

Christine's chest filled with warmth. Tammy really was radiating happiness. She looked so much more relaxed than the wide-eyed young lady who had served her on the grand-opening day of the tearoom.

'Ben is one of the best people I know, Tammy, and he's equally lucky to have you looking after him. We've done our best to look out for him, but he's so independent. We even offered to take it in turns to fetch and take his cart back up that hill to his house after he'd finished for the day, but he's as stubborn as a mule and wouldn't have it.'

Tammy laughed. 'As strong as one as well. I don't know how he does it. Is this to eat in?'

Christine nodded. Yes. I'm sitting over there with Morgan.' She pointed as she spoke.

'Take a seat. I'll bring it over to you.'

'Thanks love.'

Taking the seat opposite Morgan, Christine was surprised when Morgan asked a question before she was settled. 'Well, what's this all about?'

The edges of Christine's mouth shot up with her brows. 'What do you mean? Can't a woman ask her best friend out for an early breakfast?' Morgan lifted an eyebrow, sending a ripple of creases over the one side of her brow as she tilted her head, giving Christine a look. 'Okay-okay. You know me too well.'

FINDING LOVE IN SEAGULL BAY

'I knew something was up, and I'm guessing that something is to do with the same two men we were talking about on our girly shopping trip?'

'Oh Morgan.' Christine looked around to make sure no one was listening as she leaned forward and lowered her voice. 'Knowing what you know about my mixed-up feelings and attraction for *those* men, I'll quickly regale two incidents from yesterday.' Morgan gasped. 'The first involved me helping Marcus wash a rather large puppy, which got me soaked and unbeknownst to me, turned me into a bedraggled mess, which was the exact moment Tom decided to walk in on us and catch us laughing. The look on his face. Anyone would have thought I'd plunged a dagger into his chest. He even referred to Marcus as my boyfriend until I put him right.' Morgan gasped again. 'And then after work, I showed Marcus where Katherine's house was so he could get the housing agent's number from the display board outside to enquire about renting it, and then we *just happened* to rub into Tom again.' Christine made exclamation marks with her fingers. Who was *coincidentally* taking Rosie for a walk past Katherine's house at that exact time, even though he lives on the other side of the bay, and I'm convinced it was because he'd heard us say we were meeting later on.'

[margin note: run]

Morgan's hands flew to her cheeks. 'Did Tom say anything to you the second time?'

Christine shook her head. 'No. All he said was, evening, before continuing on.'

'And what about Marcus? Did he say anything about seeing Tom again?'

'No. He just replied, evening back to him.'

Morgan placed her hands down flat on the table, spreading her fingers open. 'Okay. So me, it's obvious Tom likes you, too. He's displaying all the characteristics of a jealous lover.'

'Lover!' Christine snorted, and then looked back over her shoulders to make sure no one had heard her.

'And Marcus...' Morgan pursed her lips together. 'It's not as blatant, but by asking you to help him wash a *puppy*. I think he's also sending out hints he also likes you—more subtlety—but hints all the same.'

'It was a very large puppy, Morgan.'

'But still a puppy. And let's not forget he's a professional dog groomer, with quite a few years of experience under his belt.'

Christine chewed the inside of her mouth as she pondered Morgan's answers.

'There you are, ladies. Two orders of scrambled eggs on toast and two teas.' Tammy rested a tray down on the edge of the table as she unloaded the order. 'Enjoy.'

Morgan smiled up at Tammy. 'Thanks love.' When she was gone, she looked across at Christine. 'Question is, Christine, if you had the choice, who would you like to date? Because dating two men simultaneously is a complex dynamic that won't end well, so I suggest you take a chance on one of them.' Christine nodded. 'So...?'

Christine lifted her gaze to meet Morgans. 'So what?'

'If the opportunity comes knocking, which of them does your heart tell you to go for?'

Christine licked her lips nervously. 'My head tells me to go for Marcus...but my heart...is with Tom.'

Morgan sighed as she picked up her cutlery. 'Well, you do both deserve another chance at love, Christine.' She scooped up a forkful of egg and popped it into her mouth.

'But what if it doesn't work out, Morgan? It will ruin our friendship. Plus, I don't want his heart broken for a third time.'

As Morgan chewed, her eyes turned upwards as if she were deep in thought. She swallowed and looked directly into Christine's eyes. 'Life is for living, Christine. Don't let the *what-if's* stop you from doing just that—living. Look at my poor Bren and Tom's wife. Here one day and gone the next.' She reached across the table and grabbed one of Christine's hands. You aren't exactly getting any younger, my dear.'

Christine laughed aloud. 'I knew it was a good idea asking you for advice again.' She picked up her own cutlery and began to eat. Morgan smiled, tapped her hand on Christine's, and withdrew it to take a sip of tea.

*

Christine turned the salon sign to open and looked at her appointment book at her first client of the day. A smile stretched her lips. Her first client was a little girl which made her happy, but it was the mother of the child that made her heart race and her tummy pinch with nerves. Tom's eldest daughter was bringing her daughter in for an appointment. If they started dating, they would be—sort of family.

Exactly to the dot the door to the salon jingled open and Francis and her daughter, Francesca walked in with smiling faces.

Christine greeted them with genuine warmth, bending over with her hands resting on her knees to be eye to eye with Francesca as she greeted her.' Hello there Francesca. I've been so excited to receive a visit from a fairy this morning. I love trimming away hair that's lost its sparkle, because fairy's need *all* of their hair to be sparkly don't they?'

Little Francesca's eyes widened, believing every word that came out of Christine's mouth. She looked up at her mommy. 'I'm a magical fairy, Mommy?'

Francis' smile stretched from ear to ear as she looked from Christine to Francesca. 'You are. You are my magical girl. Christine is going to make your hair even more beautiful. Morning Christine.'

'Good morning Francis.' Christine held her hand out and Francesca took hold of it. She led her over to a styling chair. Christine looked over to Francis. 'Mommy, can you lift your little fairy into this chair please whilst I get her a sticker to choose from?'

Francis smiled as she walked over and lifted her daughter. Christine held two stickers and mouthed silently to Francis. 'Is she allowed a sugar free lollipop?' Francis nodded. She brought her attention back to Francesca. 'Right. I have two stickers here, but to receive one, you have to tell me if you like kittens or puppies the best?'

Francesca clapped her hands together. 'Puppies! Just like Rosie, Grandpa's dog.'

Christine grinned as she tucked the kitten sticker away in her pocket and handed Francesca the puppy sticker. 'That's for being a good little fairy so far.'

Francesca giggled with delight, holding the sticker up for Francis to see. 'Puppy. Look Mommy. I got a girl puppy.'

'Oh, that's lovely, Francesca.'

Christine selected a small styling robe. 'I'm going to put a special cape on you now, Francesca. This will stop the hair that's lost its sparkle from getting stuck to your clothes when I trim it away. Do you want your mommy to hold onto your sticker a little while?' Francesca shook her head and both Francis and Christine laughed softly. 'That's okay. Hold it carefully and if you sit very still whilst I'm trimming your hair, you'll also get a special lollipop as well.'

Francesca sat ramrod straight. 'Good girl,' said Francis.

Christine picked up her brush and began to brush through Francesca's light brown waves. Her hair was as soft as silk. She turned to Francis. 'Is this still her first hair on the ends?'

Francis nodded. 'It is. I've hung on and hung on not wanting it cut off, but it's just so fly-away, and with Francesca starting full time at nursery in September, I thought it was time.'

Christine could see Francis was trying not to get emotional in front of her daughter. She nodded her understanding and smiled at Francesca's reflection as she spoke, but her words were aimed at Francis. 'Just because it's not as sparkly as the new hair anymore, it doesn't mean we want to throw it away, does it Francesca?' The little girl shook her head. 'How about I catch it and place it in a special envelope?' Francesca's eyes went wide and she smiled as she shook her head. 'Keep still then, and I'll fetch a special envelope to put it in.' Franscesca smiled and Christine turned to Francis. 'One minute.' Francis was dabbing at the corner of her eyes as she nodded.

Christine hurried into the storeroom. She had a pack of sparkly envelopes left over from Christmas when she'd sent discount vouchers to her most loyal customers. Just as she found them, she heard her shop doorbell tinkle, and then Francesca's little voice.

'Grandpa, look I'm a fairy.'

Tom's voice was soft when he replied. The way he spoke so gently to his granddaughter made Christine's heart stutter.

'Christine told me she had a special magical fairy coming in today, but I never guessed it was my own little princess. Does that mean you are a fairy princess?'

Francesca gasped. 'Wow. Yes-yes, I must be Grandpa.'

'Hello dad. What are you doing here?'

'I was just passing and I saw you through the window. Why didn't you tell me Francesca was getting her haircut? I want to be there for all her special occasions.' His voice turned softer again as he spoke to his granddaughter. 'Don't I, princess fairy?'

Christine walked back into the salon and Tom's eyes ran over her. Christine's breath caught in her throat. He was dressed casually smart again and he looked very handsome. 'Hello Tom. No work today?'

'Not today.'

There was a few seconds of silence as they stared at each other. Francis looked from her father to Christine, a small frown forming between her brows.

Christine lifted the envelope and shook it, planting a bright smile on her face. 'I found the special envelope Francesca.'

'I'm called princess fairy now, Grandpa said.'

'Oh, okay. Right, let's trim away the hair that's lost its sparkle, shall we?' Francesca nodded.

As Christine trimmed Francesca's hair, she glanced periodically at Tom and was taken aback by the love that radiated from his face as he watched his granddaughter have her first haircut. She truly believed what she'd heard when Tom had told his daughter about wanting to experience all the special first occasions with his granddaughter.

When Christine was finished, she handed the envelope of wispy hair to Francis. 'One for the memory box.'

Francis took it with a grateful smile. 'Thank you.'

Christine turned back to Francesca, took off the robe and pointed to the tub of lollies next to Tom on the counter. 'Can you bring over the lollies, Grandpa? Princess fairy needs to choose one.'

He looked at her again for the first time since he'd entered the salon and smiled with a wink, his way of thanking Christine for playing along. 'Of course I will, special sparkle stylist.'

Christine's tummy fluttered.

Chapter eleven

After watching how loving and supporting Tom had been with his granddaughter, Christine's evening had been one of contemplation. She reflected on her marriage to Sam. She'd been so in love with him. They'd met not long after she'd qualified as a hairdresser from college. It had been a whirlwind romance and engagement. Her parents had loved him just as much as she had, accepting him as the son they'd always hoped to have one day but never did. Christine wondered if fertility problems were hereditary, as it had taken years for her parents to conceive her, and try as they might, they weren't lucky a second time.

Locking up the salon, she walked around to the seafront to see if Ben was still there with his fish cart. But she wasn't surprised to see the spot he frequented daily was empty. Steering herself for the climb, she headed for the climb that would take her up to Ben's cottage.

Huffing and puffing as she made her way up the steep road,she had to rest on a wall halfway up as she always did. She'd lived in the bay all her life and when she was a child and a young teen, she could run up the steep and winding roads easily, but as she'd gotten older, the climb had become arduous and it never got any better, even if she did it daily. But the views were worth the effort, and Christine took the opportunity to gaze around and appreciate the beauty and scenery of her coastal hometown.

The view of the ocean was, as always, a joy to look at. No matter what the weather, she loved staring out at the vastness of the sea. Seagulls flew just feet above the rippling surface waves, some of them dive bombing and completely submerging, only to reappear seconds later with a fish floundering in its beak.

In the distance, Christine could see a trawler on the horizon and watched it until it was out of sight. She loved boats, and had spent many happy hours with Sam out on their small boat sailing around the harbour, but that hobby had ended with their marriage.

Bringing her gaze back to shore, she watched the last straddling holidaymakers packing away after a day of frolicking by the sea. Mothers shook out beach towels and packed bags ready to return to hotels or B 'n' B's, whilst fathers chased children with their footwear. Christine smiled and sighed to herself and then pursed her lips and turned her back on the happy scene, not wanting to be reminded of a life that could have been.

The door to Ben's wooden lean-to hut was ajar, so Christine knocked it hard before venturing inside and calling out his name. 'Ben? Are you still open for business?'

Moments later, the side door leading into his house opened and Ben appeared. 'Ahh, I thought I heard someone. Hello lass. Come for some supper for your ma and pa?'

Christine smiled when he reached for a toothpick and popped it between his lips, something he did whenever he served her in the hut. 'Yes, you know the routine, Ben. Fish on Thursdays.'

'How are they, Christine? I've been meaning to call in and see them, but with Tammy moving in and taking on Katherine's café, turning it into a tearoom, I've not had time.'

Christine nodded her head. 'Oh, they're good, Ben. As you know, they don't do much. Maybe potter around the house and the garden. And then they have their favourite TV soaps they *have* to watch.' Ben chuckled. 'The carers call in daily and I pop in a few times a week to cook their supper. So all in all, considering they are probably the oldest couple living in the bay, life is pretty decent for them.'

Ben nodded as he opened his chest freezer. 'That's good to know. Tell them I'll call on Monday evening.'

'I will.' Christine walked over to the freezer and peered in. 'What you got for me today?'

Ben reached in and withdrew three pieces of haddock. 'These have only been in there half an hour so bear that in mind when you cook them.'

'Perfect,' Christine nodded with a smile. Can you wrap them for me, please Ben?'

Ben pulled out some paper from a pile and swiftly wrapped the fish before popping them in a paper bag. 'How will you be cooking them, Christine?'

'Pan frying them, Ben.'

'Can I suggest you add garlic butter?'

'Mmmm, you're making my mouth water. How much do I owe you?'

Ben handed her the package. 'Just call it ten pounds.'

Christine withdrew the correct note and handed it to Ben with a wink. 'Keep the change.'

Ben chortled and shook his head. 'You're just as cheeky now as you were in your youth. Go on, be off with you. And don't forget to pass on my message.'

Christine grinned as she held her hand up in a farewell gesture as she walked out of the hut. 'I will. Thanks Ben. See you soon.'

*

After spending the evening with her elderly parents eating a fish supper followed by an hour in front of the TV with them, Christine helped the carers when they came in to put them to bed and then kissed them goodnight before locking up and setting home.

Her house was on the other side of the bay close to the church. Normally after leaving her parent's house, she'd head through the town, peering into shop windows and seeing if her friends who owned businesses in the bay, had changed their window displays. This evening she chose the beach route.

The sun was low in the sky, and it was still a blend of blues and pinks making the evening perfect for a beautiful walk home on the shoreline. The sound of the lapping waves eagerly drew her as she walked down the steps onto the beach and Christine slipped her feet out of her shoes and dug her toes into the sand, yelping in surprise at how quickly it had cooled, but she still enjoyed the freedom of bare feet as they sunk into the soft cool grains.

The gentle sound of the waves lured her closer to the edge of the sea and she gasped when the cool dry sand changed to wet cold sand beneath her feet. Nearing closer still to the tumbling waves, Christine found herself gathering up her dress in her fists and jumping the rush of the next tumbling wave. She giggled at her own frivolity until a clump of something slimy wrapped around her ankle and then she squealed like a child and ran back to the safety of the dry sand, only to laugh aloud at herself when she realised what she thought was a jellyfish was actually seaweed.

Continuing home, she inhaled deeply and then decided to stop walking to close her eyes and appreciate the smells and sounds surrounding her. Calm and tranquillity settled over her like a veil. She didn't know how long she was standing motionless for, but she was drawn out of her tranquil state by the faint yap of a dog up ahead. Opening her eyes, she instantly recognised the wide shoulders and confident swagger accompanied the little black and white dog.

The man up ahead halted momentarily when he spotted her and lifted his hand to wave. Christine followed suit. They met a minute later in between where they'd first spotted each other.

'Good evening Christine. It's a bit late to be out alone on the beach.'

Tom's concern was met by faint irritation. Didn't he realise she was a grown woman who'd walked this route at this time of year for over two decades?

'Not really. It's not as if I'm in the centre of a city, is it? This is Seagull Bay—not central London.'

Tom's jaw jutted out. It was clear he didn't like her reply, but as a good friend, he'd made his concern clear. 'Yes, you're right. Seagull Bay is a different world compared to a city... Still, it doesn't won't stop me from caring about your wellbeing.'

Christine's stomach fluttered. He'd admitted to caring about her—not in so many words—but he'd still admitted to it.

She looked down at Rosie whose tail was wagging frantically as she waited for Christine to acknowledge her. 'Hello Rosie. How do you like the beach?'

Rosie barked and ran around in circles. Christie laughed, and Tom joined in. 'I think she understands you, Christine.' Any tension that was there instantly disappeared. 'Are you going to Phil and Pamela's summer bar-b-q at Poppy farm this weekend?'

Christine nodded enthusiastically. 'I am. Morgan and I went shopping a few days ago for it and bought fantastic dresses. Are you going?'

'I want to go, but I don't want to be the fifth wheel and infringe on my daughters and their partners' fun. I know it's not cool for them to have their middle-aged father hanging around with them at every community function. They've had me shadowing them since the year dot.'

'Aww. You've been a wonderful father and admired from afar by many local women residents.'

Tom's brow lifted. 'Really?'

'Yes.'

'For my fathering skills?'

'Yes. I doubt there's a father in the bay more dedicated to his children and grandchildren than you.'

'That's so reassuring to hear. I've often wondered if I've stifled the girls when they were children and then cramped their style as teenagers.'

Tom's admission caused Christine to giggle. 'But they're adults now and look how good you are with Francesca.'

Tom smiled. 'Yes, but I'm still their dad and I'm guessing they don't think it's cool to hang out with their parent.' Tom licked his lips nervously. 'What if we went together?' Christine's brow lifted in surprise and Tom quickly added, 'As friends of course.'

'Well, I am going with Morgan, but you can come with us, or we can meet up with you there.'

Tom nodded, a smile tugging up the corners of his mouth. 'Yes. I'll tag along with you two if you don't mind. Then I won't look such a loner if I rock up on my lonesome.'

Christine smiled. 'Okay. Well, I'm meeting Morgan at the pub. She's driving. She's on a course of antibiotics at the moment, so she's not drinking alcohol. We're meeting at three.'

Tom nodded. 'Great.' They stood staring at each other in silence for a moment. 'Let me walk you home.'

Christine shook her head. 'Oh no. You don't have to, you've just come from that direction.'

'I don't mind. It will wear Rosie out a bit more. She's a little tinker waking in the middle of the night at the moment, playing with toys every couple of hours. It kind of reminds me of when Georgina was a baby.'

Christine nodded her head, agreeing to him accompanying her back home. 'Okay.' Her chest tightened as she imagined Tom having to deal with a toddler and a newborn baby alone whilst grieving for his wife. It must have been so terribly difficult for him losing her not long after Georgina was born, and then having to care for two small infants alone.

They walked side-by-side up the beach, Rosie in between them. Tom was still dressed in his smart clothes and his cologne tantalised Christine's senses. She was so distracted, she didn't see the broken beer bottle half-hidden in the sand and it nicked the soft skin in the inner arch of her foot.

'Ouch.' Christine's natural reaction was to grab onto Tom's arm so that she could lift her foot to examine it.

'Are you alright?'

They both looked down and saw the bottle and the small trickle of blood coming from the cut on Christine's foot, dripping onto the sand.

'I-I think it's just a nip.' Christine dropped her shoes to look inside her bag for a tissue and a plaster. She always liked to be prepared for all eventualities, but she grimaced when she remembered she'd used her plasters a few days ago whilst out with Morgan when her new shoes had rubbed her heels.

She was just about to grab the only clean tissue in her bag when she spotted a large mouth imprint on the underside of it from when she'd blotted her lipstick. She didn't want Tom thinking she was vain, so with only one free hand, she ripped off a little of the tissue and held it against the cut. It soon turned red.

'It looks bad, Christine.'

'The daft thing is Tom, it really isn't. It just won't stop bleeding. She grabbed the broken bottle and put it in her bag. 'I'd better remove this from the beach in case it cuts a small child or a dog.' She looked down at her brand new white canvas shoes that had cost a small fortune, a gift to herself when Marcus had taken on the rental of the dog grooming parlour. 'Do you mind if I hang onto your arm until we get off the beach, Tom? I don't want to ruin my shoes and I don't want to get sand in my cut either.'

Tom reached down and retrieved the shoes, passing them to Christine. 'Are you okay holding small dogs?'

Christine's brow drew together. 'Yes, why?'

'I have a better idea.'

He picked up Rosie and passed her to Christine. Stunned, she clutched both Rosie and the shoes to her chest, and before she could protest, Tom whisked her and Rosie up into his arms.

Christine shrieked, making Rosie yap. 'Sorry Rosie. It's okay.' She stroked the little dog, trying to settle her down when she was far from feeling settled herself. Her heart thundered against her chest. The intimate act embarrassed her. Tom strode onwards in the direction the beach would take her to her house, instead of heading off the beach for the road. 'Tom, you really don't have to carry me back. If you take me to the road, I can walk it back...and besides, I'm far too heavy.'

'You don't weigh a thing and I'm not having you catch an infection in that cut from the dirty pavement. You'd miss the summer bar-b-q.'

Tom had a valid point, but it didn't stop Christine from cringing inwardly. She rested against Tom's chest and it felt as hard as granite rock. He was really strong to be able to carry both Rosie and her, and was far more muscular than Christine had first given him credit when she'd secretly appraised his physique days earlier in his tight fitting t-shirt. She listened to the steady rhythm of his breathing as he carried her and was impressed by the fact he didn't appear to be physically exerting himself—a far cry from how she had sounded earlier in the evening as she'd headed to Ben's house.

The silence lengthened on and Christine searched for something to say. It wasn't often she found herself dumbstruck. She'd dreamed of being in this very same situation so many times before, only in her dreams there was no cut foot and no pets, and the man carrying her was always faceless. Christine studied Tom's jawline. Had it always been so chiselled?

In the end, it was Tom who broke the silence. 'So, what colour is your dress?'

'Huh?'

'The dress you bought for the bar-b-q?'

'Oh, it's white with a floral pattern.'

'Nice. I can't wait to see you in it.'

Christine's chest fluttered as if it had a hundred butterflies inside it. Tom headed for the gap in the dunes that led back to the road and soon they were standing outside Christine's yellow front door. Christine looked up at him.'Thank you.'

Tom gazed down into her face, his lips parting slightly. For a brief moment, Christine thought he was going to kiss her and her pulse quickened. 'Here we are.' He gently lowered her down and she handed Rosie over.

Tom took her and nuzzled his face into Rosie's fur, kissing his new pet instead. She licked his cheek in return. 'You were a good girl weren't you, my little beauty?'

Wishing she was Rosie, Christine made herself look away and down at her cut. It had already stopped bleeding. She knew she'd been right thinking it was superficial. Looking back up, she found Tom's eyes studying her, they were unreadable. 'Erm, well thank you again. I-I'll see you at the pub at three with Morgan if I don't see you before.'

He nodded, a ghost of a smile lifting the corner of his mouth. 'You will.' He turned away and strode off still carrying Rosie. Christine watched him leave. The smell of his cologne had rubbed off on her clothes and was making the butterflies soar again.

Chapter twelve

The next day, Christine found it difficult to concentrate whilst she worked. She was glad when it was time to bid farewell to her final client of the morning. Then she set about sweeping up hair.

'Earth to Christine,'

She blinked and looked up. Marcus was extending his arm, offering her a steaming mug of tea. 'I've called your name three times, but you were in a world of your own. I've made you a drink.'

Christine set the broom to one side and smiled brightly as she took the mug from him. 'Sorry. Yes, I was. I was daydreaming.'

'Gorgeous hunk, a snowy white beach and a cabana, by any chance?'

She chuckled and heat sizzled under her cheeks. 'Yes, something like that.' She went over to the sign hanging on her door and turned it around to the closed side, before settling into the customer's sofa.

Marcus sat on one of the styling chairs and met Christine's eyes in the reflection of the mirror. 'Busy morning? I hope it was okay that I sent another couple of my clients your way?'

Christine nodded. 'Yes-yes, fine. I really appreciate the extra custom to be honest. Summer is usually my busiest time, but for the last few years, it's been hard to gauge. What about you? Have you had many new clients since you've been here?'

'Blimey—yes. I'm even considering hiring someone part-time.'

Christine watched him as he spoke. No matter what time of the day, he was always immaculate in his appearance. Without realising it, she was comparing Marcus and Tom physically. A few days ago she would have been undecided who was the most handsome, but this morning, Tom was inching forward in the invisible race.

'Wow. That's exciting. I used to have the occasional helper, but as I said, it's been hard to gauge how busy I'll be these last few years, and I didn't want to pay an extra wage I couldn't afford.'

Marcus frowned slightly. 'If you don't mind me asking, doesn't your partner help out with bills if business is slow?'

Christine felt her cheeks get hotter. She could just see them now. They probably looked like lighthouse beacons. 'I've been divorced for quite some time now Marcus...I haven't dated since it was finalised.'

'Oh—I'm sorry. I didn't mean to pry.'

Christine shook her head. 'No. You weren't prying. My divorce is common knowledge.'

'What about you? Anyone special in your life?'

Marcus smiled with thin lips and Christine noticed how the smile didn't reach his eyes. 'No. It ended a while back. I'm still waiting for that *special someone* to walk into my life.'

The atmosphere had suddenly changed. 'There's always the summer bar-b-q held at Poppy farm. The whole community of Seagull Bay will be there.'

'I've heard a few of the locals talking about it. Will you be going?'

Christine's tummy did a loop-the-loop. 'Yes, I will. It's this weekend. It usually starts early so that the children can attend, but it continues until midnight. Phil, the owner of the farm, then uses his tractor and a trailer filled with hay bales to become the local free taxi.'

Marcus laughed. 'It sounds like fun.'

'It is.'

'Then I'll come as soon as I can. I have a meeting early in the afternoon, but I'll be driving. Maybe I'll get a chance of riding the trailer next year if I'm living in the bay.' His eyes sparkled with mischief as they met hers in the reflection of the mirror.

A knock on the door startled Christine and she turned to see Georgina, Tom's youngest daughter. She put her tea down and opened it. 'Hello Georgina.'

'Hi Christine. Sorry to knock like that, but I saw you and... Anyway, I thought you were open all day and I called on the off-chance you could fit me in for a cut and blow-dry. With the bar-b-q happening this weekend—I-I wanted to look my best.'

Christine smiled. 'I was just telling Marcus, the new dog groomer, all about it.' She gestured to the seated Marcus and Georgina's eyes followed. She smiled shyly at him. 'So, do you want to make an appointment or did you want me to do it now before lunch?'

'Oh erm, I don't want to put you to any trouble if you are already closed.'

Christine turned the sign around to open. 'It's no trouble at all. Come on in.'

Marcus stood up and drank the remainder of his tea in one go. 'I'll catch you later Christine. I'm going to eat lunch at Tammy's Tearoom today. Do you want anything bringing back?'

'No thanks. I brought my own lunch today.'

'No worries.'

Marcus headed to the back of the salon and to his own parlour and Christine stepped aside and motioned for Georgina to come in. She'd cut both Francis and Georgina's hair since they were little, and was grateful that most of the children from when she first opened the salon still continued to use her salon even now, as grown-ups. Only a few travelled further afield to other local salons in nearby towns or into the city to get their hair cut.

Georgina walked over to the washbasin and sat down in the chair. Christine closed the door and followed her, taking a robe and a towel on the way. Georgina held her arms out, and Christine put the robe on her before draping the towel around her shoulders.

As Georgina leaned back, placing her neck in the washbasin groove, Christine looked down into her upside-down face. 'Do you want a cold drink before I wash your hair, love?'

Georgina smiled as she shook her head. 'No thanks, I've not long had my lunch. How did you remember I don't like tea or coffee?'

Christine smiled down with genuine affection. 'I've known you since you were a toddler.' She chuckled to herself. 'Do you remember when Francis was pregnant with Francesca and she could only stomach drinking chocolate flavoured milk for about two months?'

Georgina's eyes and mouth widened in surprise. 'I'd completely forgotten about that.' She giggled. 'So that's why Francesca must like it so much.' They both laughed.

Christine gathered Georgina's long hair and placed it in the basin. She turned on the water and checked the temperature before wetting it. 'Is that too warm?'

'No, that temperature is perfect. I don't get how some people can have almost cold showers just because it's summer.'

'Ah, now that's where our opinions differ. When you get to my age, hormone changes make temperature regulation a nightmare, so I love a cool shower every now and again.'

Georgina laughed softly. 'Of really. See...that's the type of information I miss out on not having mum here.'

Christine's chest tightened. Tom was the best father in the world, but even he couldn't help his daughters with certain important *women's* issues. She wondered how he'd gotten on when his girls were of a certain age. Until then, Christine hadn't thought about *that* side of parenting. Tom had done so well raising his girls without their mother, they really were a credit to him.

'Was your dad's able to broach certain feminine subjects as you grew up?'

'He got us lots of books,' Georgina laughed softly. 'Bless him. He did the best he could.'

Christine smiled down warmly at Georgina as she visualised Tom handing over those books and the awkward look he might have had on his face. Christine massaged shampoo into Georgina's hair. 'Have you got the day off work?'

'Yes, I booked a few days off. I've been helping Francis re-decorate Francesca's bedroom. It still had baby wallpaper on the walls. Francis wanted a more grown-up theme before she started a full-time rota at school.'

'Awww. It's nice that you are still close.'

'Our relationship was a bit fractious in our teenage years, but we're as close as ever.'

'That's good. I always wished I'd had a sibling.'

Georgina laughed. 'Believe me, no you don't.' Christine laughed along with her. 'I'm only joking. I don't know what I would do if I didn't have Francis.'

'Conditioner? I also remember you don't always like it.'

'Not today thanks, Christine. I did a deep condition on my hair two nights ago. I don't know what it is, but too much conditioning leaves my hair lifeless.'

Christine dabbed the water from Georgina's hair. 'You can sit up now.' She placed a dry towel around her neck. 'Go on over to a styling chair, love.'

When Georgina was settled, Christine removed the towel and placed a cutting collar around her shoulders. She met Georgina's eyes in the reflection of the mirror. 'Just your usual cut is it?' Georgina nodded and Christine began to comb through Georgina's hair, before sectioning it to trim it.

'Dad's been talking a lot about you recently, Christine.'

The statement made Christie's stomach flutter, but she played off the comment with a joke. 'I'm not surprised. He's probably been telling you how hard I worked him while he was doing the re-fit for the dog grooming room.' She lifted her head and smiled at Georgina's reflection.

'He was in his element doing that.'

'That's good to hear because I was more than a little concerned for him when he first took on the job, being as it was so soon after his split with Jenny.'

Georgina's face screwed up at her name. 'Ugh. I really wanted to give her a piece of my mind, but Francis warned me off saying it wasn't any of my business. But when it's our dad getting hurt, I just want to protect him. Do you know what I mean, Christine?'

Christine nodded. 'I do, love.'

They remained silent for a few minutes, each lost in their own thoughts as Christine went about her task.

'He mentioned something about you and him going to the bar-b-que.'

Christine stopped cutting for a moment and blinked at Georgina, unsure how to answer after her revelation about wanting to get in touch with Jenny. 'Erm yes. He's tagging along with Morgan and me.' She couldn't help but notice the look of relief that washed over Georgina's face.

'Oh, so the *three* of you are going together?' Christine nodded and busied herself with Georgina's hair. 'That's a relief. I don't mean this to sound mean or anything, Christine, but I was worried he was about to fall into a rebound relationship to get over the break-up with Jenny. So, just to clarify. There are no romantic intentions between you and my dad?'

Christine frowned and shook her head. Her heart was thundering in her chest and it was difficult to contain her disappointment. She'd been building up the idea of a possibility of having a relationship with Tom that was so much more than a mere friendship, but Georgina and possibly Francis too, didn't seem to think their father getting involved again was a very good idea. 'No-no. We are just good friends.'

Georgina sighed. 'I thought as much, but I still wanted to check. I really don't want him getting hurt again, Christine. It really knocked it out of dad when Jenny dumped him by text just days before their holiday cruise.'

Christine forced a smile, but inside she was gutted. 'I don't want Tom, Francis, or you to get hurt again either.' She squeezed Georgina's shoulder. 'We'll look out for your dad's best interests together, shall we?'

Georgina returned the smile. 'Thanks Christine, I wished I had a female relative like you.'

Christine's stomach pinched. 'And I wished I had loving daughters like you girls. Tom is a very lucky man.'

*

After Georgina had left the salon, Christine turned the sign to closed. She felt as though she'd had the wind knocked out of her. Tom and Christine had been building a lovely rapport over the last few weeks, but now she felt as if her world had turned on its axis.

There could never be any romance between them now. She would never chance hurting those dear girls if things between Tom and her didn't work out. What was she thinking? A romance with a friend she'd known for decades was an absurd notion, anyway.

Taking off her overall, she decided she'd finish early. There were no other clients booked in for the afternoon, anyway. She'd go home and have a long soak in the bath and maybe a drink or two to mourn a relationship that was never going to be. She looked at the till and puffed out her cheeks. The cashing up could wait until tomorrow. She just wasn't in the mood. She spotted a box of chocolates one of her regulars had brought in for her next to the till. She'd been trying to cut down before the bar-b-q to ensure her new dress fit her better.

Grabbing the box of chocolates and her bag, she headed for the door. 'What does it matter anymore?'

Just as she was locking the shop door an image of Marcus came into her mind. Maybe fate was trying to tell her something. She looked down at the chocolates. Still, a few wouldn't hurt.

Act 3 - Chapter thirteen

Standing in front of the full-length mirror in her bedroom, Christine smoothed her hands down over her hips. The fifties style swing dress paired with shoes to match looked divine.

Glancing over at her bedside table to the box of chocolates she'd brought home from the salon to accompany the glass or three of alcohol she'd downed to help drown her sorrows, a faint smile crossed her lips. Just three were missing. It was a commendable amount considering the low mood she'd been in since coming to terms with the fact that Tom and her were never going to date.

Today however, she needed to return to the carefree positive mindset she was in before she'd started to get fanciful ideas about Tom and her becoming more than just good friends.

Picking up her favourite perfume, she aimed it ahead of her and squirted twice before stepping into the mist. Her make-up was a touch more than the natural look she wore daily at work and she'd spent almost an hour on her hair. With small studded quartz earrings and a fine chain with a drop-quartz pendant, she was ready. Picking up a small clutch bag and a cardigan, she headed downstairs and out of the front door.

The Cheese Wedge and Pickles was only a short distance away, and with every step she took bringing her closer to it, her heart beat quicker. In her head, she'd rehearsed how she would greet Tom and how she should chat with him, thinking carefully about what they could talk about. She'd never had to do this before. Her friendship with Tom was decades old. Their conversation had always flowed freely, but Georgina's innocent and indirect revelation yesterday had immediately had to make her do a U-turn with her growing feeling for Tom.

Trying to empty her mind to stop over-thinking her greeting with Tom, she concentrated on her surroundings. A lot of the shops that were usually open today had closed early. The same sign stuck to their windows with blue tack or cello tape written in different ways, but with the same message.

> **Closing early**
>
> August 13th.
>
> Open as normal
>
> August 14th.
>
> Sorry for any inconvenience.

The same signs had been displayed all day yesterday. The pub, the fish and chip shop and, as far as she was aware, Tammy's Tearoom would be closed this afternoon and evening. The holidaymakers who relied on them for their suppers had been forewarned and would have needed to prepare for an alternative way of feeding their families. Christine guessed the next seaside town or village would see extra custom tonight.

The afternoon sun shone high in the sky and the cardigan Christine had brought with her seemed unnecessary, but she knew as soon as it began to set later on, it would turn chilly up at the farm where the summer bar-b-q was to be held.

She saw Mrs Klein from Bell, Book & Table, just about to climb into a taxi with her husband. Christine raised her hand and waved, calling out loud enough for her to hear. 'Are you off to the bar-b-q Mrs Klein?'

Mrs Klein turned around and waved back. 'Yes, see you there.'

Christine's smile was still blazing on her face when she rounded the corner to The Cheese Wedge and Pickles, but the sight that greeted her stopped her in her tracks. Tom was talking to Morgan and he looked hot—and not in a temperature way.

He was wearing a white shirt rolled up at the sleeves underneath a brown suede waistcoat that was buttoned up, accentuating his slim waist and making his big shoulder look even wider. He'd teamed them with blue jeans, a brown belt and boots.

Christine gulped. Tom had a day's worth of stubble, which made him look even more ruggedly handsome. Morgan saw her first. 'Morning Christine. You look beautiful. You certainly chose the right dress.'

Christine smiled warmly at her friend and in her peripheral vision could see Tom checking her out. 'Morning Morgan. Thank you. So do you. I love the way you've styled your hair.'

'I can't lie. It was Pippa who did it. She called in to get a piece of her mum's jewellery to wear for the bar-b-q and sort of took over.' Morgan laughed as she dabbed at her hair with the heel of her hand. She dipped her head in Tom's direction. 'And what about Tom? Doesn't he look dapper?'

Their eyes met and her chest fluttered. 'Yes. Very...handsome.'

The side of Tom's mouth hitched up. 'I'll be the envy of the men attending the bar-b-que with stunners like you two on either arm.'

Morgan chuckled and swept his comment away with her hand. 'Get away with you, you old charmer.'

Tom's smile grew wider. 'Hey, less of the old, thank you very much.'

Morgan motioned for them to follow as she turned around. 'I'll just fetch Brett. He got a bit weepy when Pippa was looking through Maria's jewellery.'

Tom crossed his arms in front of his chest, and Chrisitne thought it must be a protective gesture for himself whenever someone who had passed over was mentioned. 'Did he still think Maia was alive?'

Morgan shook her head. 'No. Thankfully his dementia isn't that bad. There's only been one time in the last three months when he did.' She passed a key to Tom. 'Here. You and Christine can get in the car while you wait.'

Tom took the keys. 'Okay.' They both watched Morgan as she walked away before Tom turned around to face Christine. His eyes wandered over her. 'You look gorgeous by the way.'

Christine could feel the blush materialising, but could do nothing to stop it. 'Thank you.'

He held his arm out to the side, gesturing for her to go ahead. 'Shall we?'

Christine nodded and began to walk on jittery legs towards Morgan's car. It beeped and Tom stepped in front of her to open the door. 'Thank you.' She climbed in and smoothed down her dress as Tom shut the door and then tried her best not to stare at him as he walked around the front of the car to get in beside her.

As soon as he shut his door, his cologne filled the car's interior, making Christine's heartbeat all the faster. They each turned their heads to look at each other. Christine suddenly felt very coy in such close quarters and gave Tom a small smile. Normally one never to be shy to make conversation, she found herself rendered dumb.

The atmosphere inside the car was electric, so when Tom slowly lifted a hand towards her, Christine shrunk back slightly, baffled by what he was about to do. Could it be that he wanted to run his hand over her hair before he kissed her?

'You have a feather. Let me just—' His fingers barely touched her, but Christine felt as though she'd been zapped with electricity. Her pulse quickened. 'See.' He held the feather in front of her face. 'Pesky seagulls.'

He turned around and opened the door to throw the feather out, which gave Christine a moment to gather herself and draw in a long breath to steady her racing heart. Brett and Morgan appeared and got into the car.

Brett turned around and offered his hand to Tom. 'Good day young sir. I barely recognised you. Have you swallowed a magic pill to regain your youth? I thought for a moment you were Pippa's fiancé, Oliver.'

Tom chuckled as he took Brett's hand for a single shake in greeting. 'I'll take that indirect compliment.'

Christine leaned forward and kissed Brett's cheek. 'Hello Brett. Are Pippa and Oliver making their own way there?'

'Yes. They are contemplating taking the dogs. Phil and Pamela have said all dogs are welcome as long they are kept on leashes at all times. I think they are providing food for pets as well.'

Morgan started the engine. 'Everyone buckled up?' They quickly put their belts on and set off for Poppy farm.

*

Poppy farm was already a buzz of activity as Morgan parked her car in the small field Phil the farmer had designated as a carpark for the day. As Christine climbed out of the car, the smell of cooking meat wafted in the air making her tummy rumble.

The excited squeals of delight and laughter coming from a group of children who were navigating a hay maze were almost drowning out the folk band who were playing not far from a long table laden with food. Some of the bay's residents were already up and dancing and Christine's face lit up at the joyous scene. There hadn't been a summer bar-b-q at Poppy farm for a few years, ever since Brett's wife Maria had passed and to see everyone here again smiling and happy was soul lifting.

'Shall we get a drink first?' said Tom.

Brett laughed. 'You read my mind.' He looked at Morgan and Christine. 'Ladies? What can we get for you?'

'Just a cordial for me, Brett,' said Morgan.

'Christine, what would you like?' asked Tom, and at that moment, she felt as though this was becoming a date. Her stomach pinched and she looked around for Tom's daughters. 'Christine?'

'Oh erm. I'll have a lager please.' She watched them walk away.

Morgan called after them. 'We're going to find some seats.' She turned her attention back to Christine. 'Who were you looking for? It isn't Marcus by any chance is it? Not when you have a *very* handsome man waiting on you at this precise moment?'

Christine linked her arm through her friends. 'You are too astute for your own good, *Miss Marples*.' Morgan laughed as Christine guided her over to where the tables and chairs were.

They sat down and Morgan looked at Christine. 'Was I right then? Were you looking for Marcus?'

Christine shook her head. 'No. I was looking for Francis and Georgina.'

A deep crease appeared between Morgan's brows. 'Tom's girls? Why?' The crease disappeared and a ripple of lines formed on her forehead as her brow rose. 'Are you going to ask them if it's okay to date their dad?'

Christine grimaced. 'No. Although after seeing how gorgeous he looks today I wish I were... Georgina called in on the off chance for a cut and blow-dry. She was telling me in not so many words how Francis and she didn't want to see their dad upset again by more dating going wrong. She asked me if I was going with Tom to the bar-b-q. I obviously told her he was tagging along with both of us. That answer seemed to put her mind at rest.' Christine screwed up her nose as she grimaced again. 'I can't do it, Morgan. Even though the chemistry between us is undeniable, I can't date Tom. He's been a friend for over two decades. What if it didn't work out? It would ruin our friendship and the lovely relationships I have with Francis and Georgina. I might never get to see little Francesca again.'

Morgan sighed. 'I know what you mean, but it could also go the other way. Tom and you might be the next couple in the bay to get married after Pippa and Oliver.'

Christine spluttered a laugh. 'That's way too much over-thinking, Morgan.' She hadn't seen Brett and Tom's arrival as they placed the drinks down on the table.

'What's my wonderful sister-in-law been over-thinking about this time?' chuckled Brett.

Christine widened her eyes as she looked at Morgan. 'Oh nothing. You know me, Brett. I analyse everything,' replied Morgan.

Tom was still standing and he took a long drink of his pint of beer before placing it on the table and holding his hand out to Christine. 'Want to take a spin? I know you like this tune because I heard you singing along to it when I was fitting out the dog grooming room.'

The folk band was playing a recent *George Ezra* hit. From the corner of her eye, Christine could see Morgan watching her reaction. She shook her head. 'We've only just got here Tom. I need to acclimatise first.'

Tom shrugged with a smile. 'Fair enough, but make sure you add me to your dance card.'

Christine smiled sweetly at Tom, but her insides were churning. As much as she'd love nothing better than to be held in Tom's strong arms, she had no intention of dancing with him and leading him on—giving Francis and Georgina ideas after she'd told Georgina they were coming here just as friends. What if the dance was the moment Tom was to reveal his feelings? She wouldn't be able to contain her happiness—her own feelings would be as evident to everyone who was watching them as the nose on her face.

She got to her feet, holding her drink. 'Please excuse me everyone. I'll be back shortly. I just need to have a word with Mrs Klein, I won't be long.'

She strode away with her heart pounding and her nerves frazzled. Plus, she needed a respite from Tom's intoxicating cologne and the chemistry zapping between them.

Christine walked over to Mrs Klein and her husband and fell into a friendly conversation that she was taking part in, body only. Her mind was elsewhere, and she couldn't stop her eyes from periodically glancing in Tom's direction to see if he had stopped staring at her. But every time she looked, his admiring gaze only added more butterflies to the million that were going crazy inside her chest.

It startled her when her nearly empty glass of lager was pulled from her hand mid-sentence from behind. She turned around and was immediately pulled into someone's arms who commenced to turn them in circles as he whisked them towards the part of the field where everyone was dancing.

Once Christine got over the shock, she looked up to see who she was dancing with. Marcus's white, toothy grin greeted her. 'Surprise! I decided to reschedule my meeting. I've come earlier rather than later..'

'Marcus. I-I wasn't going to dance today.'

'Oh? Why not? You are a fabulous dancer.' He smiled at the other dancers, directing his statement at them this time. 'No left feet to see here, folks.' A couple Christine recognised who'd recently brought their three Alsatians to Ruff to Regal, laughed aloud at his comment.

Christine could feel panic rising in her chest. 'I just didn't, that's all.'

She tried to look for Tom as Marcus twirled her around. Instead, she saw Georgina who waved as she tilted her head to one side and cooed at Marcus and her. Then she locked eyes with Tom. His jaw jutted out and his arms were crossed in front of his chest again, but this not, not to protect his feelings, his body language clearly showed he was annoyed. Christine dancing with Marcus had obviously upset the apple—but it wasn't her doing. She glanced back at Georgina who was still smiling as she watched them dance. Maybe it was for the best.

Chapter fourteen

Christine was trimming Mrs Calloway's hair and listening to her rendition of the bar-b-q. She was going from one Seagull Bay resident to the next, telling Christine what she'd observed about them at the bar-b-q. Christine was only half-listening. Her mind had been on Tom from the moment her alarm had gone off that morning. It was only when Mrs Calloway mentioned Morgan and she did her ears pick up.

'Yes, and as well as you declining a dance from Tom, so did Morgan when Ned asked her to dance. I did see you dance with Marcus though, you lucky beggar. He's a very good dancer. Do you think he's had lessons?'

Christine ignored Mrs Calloway's question to ask one of her own. 'Ned asked Morgan to dance?'

'Yes. Didn't she tell you? Although I suppose she didn't get a chance because you didn't spend much time with her, Brett or Tom after dancing with Marcus, did you? How did you get back to the bay? Did you get the tractor trailer? Because I didn't see you on the first run. That's the one I came back on.'

Christine nodded with a ghost of a smile. She was mortified. What must Morgan think of her? Every time she'd made a move to go and grab Morgan to pull her away and explain what was going on, someone from the bay was sitting in her seat chatting to Brett and her. Tom had also left the table and had threaded his way through the bay's residents, trying to get closer to her, but she'd moved on whenever she'd seen him. After seeing how happy Georgina was when she'd danced with

Marcus, she didn't want to risk tilting the boat and being seen chatting and dancing with her dad.

Mrs Calloway was silent, which was unusual for her, and it pulled Christine from her reveries. She was looking at Christine's reflection with her eyebrows raised questioningly.

'Oh erm. I came back on the second trailer run.'

'Ah, okay.'

The doorbell jingled and Suzie from the florist shop came in holding a gigantic bouquet. The flora from it filled the salon. Suzie's grin stretched from ear to ear. 'Christine, love. A delivery for you?'

Christine's jaw dropped. 'For me?' She could tell from the size of Suzzie's grin, she was excited for Christine, possibly because she knew who the sender was. She handed Christine the bouquet and tapped the side of her nose as she glanced in Mrs Calloway's direction. 'Don't worry, love. I'll not let anyone find out who the sender is.' She winked before she left.

Mrs Calloway turned in her chair trying to look for a greeting card on the bouquet, but Christine kept it turned into her chest. 'Ooo! Christine. You must have made a big impression on someone at the bar-b-q.'

'Cuppa, Mrs Calloway? I won't be long. I'm just going to put these in water.'

Mrs Calloway opened her mouth to say something, but Christine turned around quickly and headed for the tea station in the stockroom before she could answer..

Her heart pounded and her hands trembled as she set the bouquet down and pulled the small envelope off the plastic holder, protruding out of the stalks. There was no message on the envelope and she swiftly tore it open and pulled out the card.

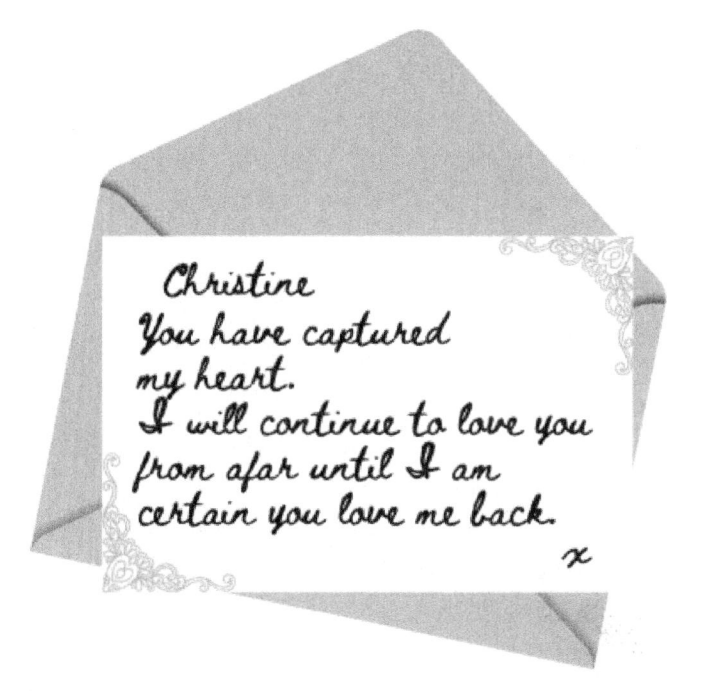

> Christine
> You have captured my heart.
> I will continue to love you from afar until I am certain you love me back.
> x

Her breath caught in her throat. Someone *loved* her. She studied the cursive writing, trying to place it. But she didn't recognise it. She lifted the card to her nose and inhaled.

The door to the storeroom opened, and Marcus appeared. An enormous grin lit up his face when he saw the bouquet. He went over to it and studied the arrangement. 'Clematis, eryngium, pink lillies, orchids, peony roses, hydrangeas. Some of my favourite flowers.' He turned to face Christine. 'You are a lucky girl. Someone must have spent a small fortune on you.'

He winked and placed two mugs in the sink. 'I'll come back in a few minutes. Give you time to put those beauties in water.'

He smiled and left. Christine was even more confused than she'd been a moment ago when she was certain the bouquet had come from Tom. How would Marcus know so many of the flower names from the bouquet? Unless they were from him.

Christine pulled her mobile phone from out of her pocket and texted Morgan.

Are you free to
meet up for lunch?
My treat? x

A reply came back almost instantly.

Yes. Where? X

Christine wanted to talk somewhere private.

I'll get us something.
Meet me by the steps
down to the beach at
12:30. X

Morgan replied.

Okay. See you soon. X

Christine put the phone and card back in her pocket, switched on the kettle and then filled up a jug with water, placing the bouquet in. She'd left Mrs Calloway alone for long enough. Fetching a clean mug from the cupboard, she quickly made a cup of tea and hurried back into the salon. She placed the tea down and continued trimming Mrs Calloway's hair.

'So? Who were they from?' Mrs Calloway's eyes were wide with expectation.

Christine was waiting for this question. 'The card didn't say.'

'Oooo! A secret admirer. How exciting.'

'Hmm.' Christine didn't say another word and concentrated on the task at hand. When Mrs Calloway wasn't looking, she glanced her way. She could see the cogs behind her eyes turning and she sighed inwardly. Soon, all the residents of Seagull Bay would know about the flowers and the secret sender.

*

With a bag in one hand loaded full of all sorts of goodies from Tammy's Tearoom, and a cardboard tray holding two special coffees in the other, Christine headed for the steps at the far right of the bay. Morgan and she had often met up by them often over the years to put the world to rights.

Morgan had her back against a wall with her hands crossed and resting on the head of her walking stick, watching Christine's approach. Christine smiled warmly at her friend and she was relieved when Morgan smiled back. It was a good start. At least Christine now knew Morgan wasn't angry at her for not spending much time with her at the bar-b-que.

She opened her mouth to apologise, but Morgan held her hand up to stop her. 'Don't worry. I read you like a book at the bar-b-q. I knew you were avoiding Tom after Marcus grabbed you to dance. I did my best to point out to Tom how Marcus had surprised you, dragging you to dance, but I think he saw it with his own eyes, anyway. Neither one was very far from your side all night. I don't know what you've done to those men, but you've certainly cast a spell over them. I really can't decide which one is more smitten with you.'

Christine sighed and closed her eyes. 'Thank goodness you aren't angry with me, and you didn't take me not sitting by you personally.'

Morgan flicked the comment away with the back of her hand. 'Never mind about that. Did you not just hear what I just said about the two most handsome and eligible men in Seagull Bay being smitten with you?'

Christine gestured for them to sit down. 'I did.' She placed down the coffees and then pulled out a clean towel from the salon and spread it out on the step in between them and began to withdraw the yummy delicacies she'd purchased for their lunch. There were mini pasties, mini quiches, and other delights.

'Oh. I almost forgot.' She pulled out a box and opened it up. It contained two slices of homemade cake. A red velvet slice for Christine, and a coffee and walnut slice for Morgan.

Morgan eyed the delights. 'My mouth's watering. I'm glad I skipped breakfast now.' A light-hearted chuckle tumbled from Christine's mouth.

'Tuck in!' commanded Christine.

They didn't speak for the first five minutes as they ate. Christine looked down at the beach, people watching. She never tired of watching how couples interacted with their children, smiling to herself when she saw a young mum parenting the way she would have parented if she'd been lucky enough to have children.

Sandcastles, some completed and others only half built lined the beach, as laughing children with happy faces knelt beside them or frolicked in the sea in brightly coloured swimsuits, their families not far away or lying next to them.

Some kept a watchful eye on their precious offspring. Some were asleep and some read paperbacks. It was a perfect beach day.

'Who are you more attracted to now after the bar-b-q?'

Morgan's question dragged her back to reality. Christine swallowed the remaining food in her mouth and turned to face her friend. 'Hmm, well there's been a few developments I need to tell you about.' Morgan popped a mini quiche into her mouth and lifted an eyebrow. 'Georgina was watching me at the bar-b-q. I think she was making sure I didn't dance with her dad. So you can imagine after what she said to me in the salon, I'm extremely dubious about interacting too intimately with Tom.' Christine looked pointedly at Morgan. 'She clearly doesn't want her father to get hurt again, does she?.'

'Ahhh. That's not good.'

'And then this morning, when I was cutting Mrs Calloway's hair—of all people. A very large and expensive looking bouquet was delivered to the salon.'

Morgan gasped. 'From who?'

Christine pulled the card from her pocket and handed it to Morgan. 'I have no idea.'

Morgan read the note quietly and gasped again. 'He's going to continue to *love you* until he knows you love him back. Oh my goodness. You know what this means don't you?'

Christine shook her head. 'No. What?'

'You are going to have to hint about your feelings to the one you like the most and hope they come clean and admit to sending the flowers.'

Christine groaned and looked out at the shimmering sea as she watched the seagulls swooping down to it. 'Why can't life be as uncomplicated as it is for the gulls?'

'Who said they have uncomplicated lives?'

Christine looked back at Morgan. 'Do you know what else Mrs Calloway saw? It must have intrigued her for her to mention it to me.'

Morgan picked up her slice of cake and held it in front of her mouth. Her eyes rolled. 'I don't know...shock me.' She opened her mouth wide and took a huge bite.

'She was curious as to why you turned down a dance with Ned.'

Morgan almost choked. Christine picked up Morgan's coffee and quickly handed it to her. She watched her friend cough and chew, her eyes watering before she swallowed and gulped down her coffee.

'Crikey. Doesn't anything go unnoticed?'

'So what's the story with you and Ned? You kept that quiet.'

Morgan shook her head vehemently. 'There is no story. Or at least, there wasn't one until Mrs Calloway saw something that no one else saw, including Ned and me.'

Christine hollered with laughter. 'You do realise, you and I are going to be the talk of the bay for the next few days until something more scandalous unfolds?'

Morgan grinned. 'Whatever makes her happy. We all need something to look forward to and get us out of bed each day, and for Mrs Calloway, that just happens to be everyone else's lives in the bay.' Christine nodded in agreement. 'Right, I'd better be off. I have the hotel accounts to sort out this afternoon.'

Christine got to her feet and then helped Morgan get up. 'Ugh, rather you than me. I hate sorting out my accounts.' She picked up the towel with everything on it and duped it into the bag the food had come in. 'I'll sort this little lot out when I get back to the salon.'

Linking arms with Morgan again, they slowly made their way back. Metres from The Cheese Wedge and Pickles, Morgan and Christine said their goodbyes. Morgan headed for the pub and Christine, for the salon.

Just as she was unlocking the door, her salon phone began to ring. She rushed in and answered it. 'Good afternoon, Christine's. How can I help you?'

'Hello Christine. It's Katherine.'

'Katherine. How wonderful to hear your voice. How are things? Have you settled in?'

'Everything is working out fine. Mother isn't half as cantankerous as I thought she was going to be.' Katherine's soft chuckle warmed Christine's heart. She'd missed hearing it. 'How are you?'

'Fine. I've just come from taking my lunch with Morgan.'

'Oh, you've just reminded me. I need to call her next. And how are you getting on with your new tenant? What's he like?'

Christine wanted to say handsome, intelligent, and the dream tenant. She opted for, 'He's lovely. I couldn't have wished for anyone better.'

'That's good to hear, because he's enquired about renting my house.'

'That was going to be the next thing to tell you, Katherine. I told him about it, and I showed him the exterior of the house so we could get the estate agent's phone number from the board outside.'

'Ah, okay. Then knowing that, would you do me a huge favour Christine?'

'Of course. Anything Katherine.'

'Would you show Marcus around the house tomorrow evening?'

Christine's gut pinched. 'Yes, you can rely on me to do my best to sell it to him.'

Katherine chuckled again. 'I really appreciate that, Christine. You can get my set of keys from Tammy. I'll ring her after I've spoken to Morgan to let her know you'll be calling in after them.'

'Is tomorrow evening after work okay to show Marcus around?'

'Whatever's best for the both of you. I'll let you sort it out with him.' Christine heard a frail voice calling Katherine's name in the background. 'Go to go, Christine, but I'll call you a day after tomorrow to see how things went with the viewing.'

'No worries, love. Speak to you soon. Bye-bye.'

'Bye Christine.'

Christine thought about the house viewing. Would she choose Marcus and ask for a hint of something more happening between them while they had no interruptions? Sighing deeply, she didn't know. She was still carrying a torch for Tom.

Chapter fifteen

The next day, Christine didn't see anything of Marcus, but he'd already forewarned her he had a busy day and would meet her at the side gate after closing time so they could walk up to Katherine's house together.

Christine herself was busy and didn't even have a chance to think about Marcus or Tom. That was until, about forty minutes until closing time. She was just coming back from using the bathroom, when she almost jumped out of her skin when she saw Tom sitting on the customer waiting couch in the salon.

'Tom. You startled me. I never heard the doorbell jingling.'

He looked up from the magazine he was flipping through, closed it and placed it on top of the pile before giving her a thin smile.

'I can assure you, it did.'

Christine noted he was wearing his work clothes. His stubble was even longer. She'd never seen it this long before, even after he'd been dumped by Jenny. 'To what do I owe the pleasure? Surely it's not another haircut already?' She really hoped he wasn't here to ask the reason why she'd avoided him at the bar-b-q. He looked forlorn. Was he the one who'd sent the flowers? Christine was still having doubts about Marcus.

Tom shook his head. 'I just wanted your opinion.'

'Oh? On what?'

'Jenny.' Christine felt her shoulders drop. The dial twisted again. This time turning her opinion 90% in favour of Marcus sending the bouquet. 'I'm considering contacting her.'

'What's brought this on? I thought you'd drawn a line under that failed relationship.'

His intense stare when he replied sent a shiver down Christine's back. 'If it's the only relationship I'll have any success at obtaining, I'm going to do everything in my power to get it back.'

Christine sighed heavily and sank into a styling chair, turning it to face Tom. She was disappointed. Tom's admission literally 99% confirmed the flowers weren't from him. 'I think you are making a big mistake, Tom.'

He leaned forward and his eyes pierced hers. 'Am I though, Christine? Is there any way of convincing me of this?'

She was certain he was challenging her, but why? Unless...the reason was the 1%.

'It's time to move on or stay single, Tom. As you know, I've not dated anyone since Sam and I got divorced. But what you don't know is the reason why we divorced, because I've only ever told Morgan and Katherine.' Christine's heart was pounding. 'I adored every hair on Sam's? head. We were so happy and dedicated to each other. Even when I found out I couldn't have children, Sam told me it didn't matter. I tried to persuade him to adopt, but he convinced me I was all he ever wanted. After a while, I accepted that and we lived to please each other. We were in our own happy little bubble.' She inhaled deeply and slowly released her breath. 'But that bubble burst when I found out Sam had been cheating on me...and worse, he's gotten the woman he'd been living a double life with, pregnant.' Tom inhaled quickly. 'So, we divorced and I slapped a smile on my face so I could get on with my life. But deep down, I was devastated, and it took me a long time to fully trust men again.'

Tom slid forward to the edge of his seat. 'Christine. Wh-why didn't you tell me?'

Christine moved to the edge of her seat. 'Tom. You were going through your own heartache. There was no way I was going to burden you with mine as well.'

Tom rubbed his forehead. 'That explains so much. I always thought you just weren't interested in starting another relationship.' He dropped his hand, his eyes searching hers, and Christine felt as if he were stripping her soul bare. 'I have something to admit to you, Christine.' Christine licked her lips. She could actually feel her pulse throbbing in her neck. 'I've admired you from afar for so many years.' Her heart shot up into her throat. 'I dated Jenny because I was lonely. That was the only reason. Really, I wanted you.'

Christine gasped. 'Me?'

Tom nodded. 'Then when things ended between Jenny and me, you were so understanding about the break-up, giving me advice and letting me cry on your shoulder. I found a way to talk to you whenever I got a chance because I knew you wouldn't turn me away. It was the closest I'd gotten to you in years. But then, when I saw a rapport developing between Marcus and you and I didn't know what to do. But there was only one thing to do. I stepped up a gear and began to give out hints of how I felt about you. I-I tried to dance with you at the bar-b-q, but my plan didn't work. Every time I got closer to you, you disappeared.'

Christine shook her head, wanting to explain her actions. 'I know, it was really busy—'

Tom cut her off. 'I'm sorry, but I need to ask you this before I lose my nerve, Christine.' Christine felt as if the oxygen had been sucked from the room. 'I know we've been friends for a long-long time, but will you go on a date with me?'

Christine was flabbergasted. Her mouth opened and closed. How could she answer? Her heart screamed yes, but her head screamed no. She had to think of the bigger picture. She had to think about Francis and Georgina.

She jumped to her feet, shaking her head. 'I-I'm sorry Tom...but I can't.' She turned on her heels and walked to the back of the salon on legs that felt as if they had lost their bones. Without looking back, she said, 'Can you turn the sign around to closed on your way out, please?'

Inside the safety of the storeroom she held onto the edge of the sink. She was shaking. Other than falling for Sam, she was sure she just made the biggest mistake of her life.

Marcus opened the door and peered inside. 'Are you read—' he strode into the storeroom and held Christine by the shoulders, his eyes narrowing with concern. 'Are you okay? You are as white as snow.'

Christine nodded. 'Yes. I'm fine. Thank you for your concern. I just came over a little dizzy, is all. I think I just need a cup of tea before we go.'

'With a spoonful of sugar, too. Go and sit down. I'll make it and bring it out to you.'

Christine hadn't heard the tinkle of the doorbell yet, notifying her of Tom leaving and her gut clenched at the suggestion of confronting him again. 'If it's okay. I'll just wait here. My legs are feeling a little weak.'

'Yes. Of course. Do what's best for you.' The tinkle of the door bell in her salon drew both of their attention. 'I think you might have a customer.' He held his palms up to her. 'Wait here. I'll tell them to come back tomorrow.' He disappeared out of the door before Christine could object. Moments later, he was back again. 'Strange. There was no one there and your sign says you are closed anyway.'

Christine just shrugged.

*

Leaving Tammy's Tearoom together after obtaining the keys for Katherine's house, Christine and Marcus made their way there.

As they walked side-by-side, she could feel his eyes burning into her profile. She turned her head to look at him. 'What is it?'

He grinned and shook his head. 'I'm just happy that you are back to your old rosy-cheeked self again.'

Christine returned the smile. 'It was that magic tea that did it...and less of the old thank you very much.'

They were still chuckling as they reached Katherine's house. Christine handed Marcus the keys. 'Not feeling well again?' His voice was edged with concern as he took the keys.

'No, I feel fine. I thought it would be nice for you to open up and get a feel of the place as soon as you push open the door.'

Marcus grinned and headed for the door, talking back over his shoulder to Christine as he put the key in the lock. 'I like your way of thinking—it's better to do things up close than afar.'

What he said halted Christine in her tracks, it was similar phrasing to what was on the note from the bouquet of flowers. He unlocked the door and went in. A few seconds later, Christine followed and closed the door behind her. Marcus stood in the hallway with his hands on his hips.

'Well? What are your first impressions?' she asked him.

He turned around to face her with a beaming smile. 'Really-really good. It's a little smaller than I'm used to, and the décor is obviously not to my taste, but there's a very homely feel to the place.'

'I'll wait in the kitchen for you until you've checked out the place. Any questions, just shout.'

Marcus nodded. 'It feels like Christmas and this is a present I'm unwrapping.'

Christine grinned as she watched him head for the first rung of the stairs. She wandered into the kitchen and opened the door of the refrigerator which had been left slightly ajar, checking there was no mould growing. Katherine had meticulously cleaned it after she'd emptied it and turned it off, leaving the door open a few inches. She tried to concentrate as she investigated it, millimetre by millimetre, but her mind swung back and forth between Tom and Marcus.

She sighed and screwed her eyes closed. Why was she beating herself up? Did she have to start dating again? Wasn't it better to stay single? But an ache in the centre of her chest that hadn't been there before, gave her a reply. She remembered the flowers and the message that came with them. And of course, there was the admission of love for her, which at this moment in time, Christine was 99% sure had come from Marcus.

'I love it…and I can be closer to what matters to me if I rent it. I'm going to take it.'

Christine spun around to see Marcus leaning against the doorframe, watching her. That was it. She had reached 100% confirmation. He was clearly referring to her when he said he would be closer to what matters to him. She needed to take Morgan's advice. She was going to hint at doing something together that could lead on to dating.

'Great. I'm pleased for you.' Her heart felt as though it might jump clean out of her chest. It was now or never. Her mouth had suddenly gone dry. 'What say we go and see a movie to celebrate?' She swallowed hard. 'Go on a date?'

Marcus's eyes widened and he took a couple of steps towards her. Christine licked her lips and braced herself for the first kiss.

Marcus cupped her cheeks and upturned her face, gazing intently into her eyes. 'Oh Christine. I'm so sorry if I've given you the wrong signals.' Her stomach felt as though it had dropped into her feet. 'I like you…really, I do…but, just as friends.' Christine stepped back and Marcus's hands fell to his sides. His rejection stung more than she thought it would. His eyes fleeted over her face. 'You are a very attractive woman, but—'

Christine held up her hands, the palms facing Marcus as she shook them. 'No-no it's fine. I'm sorry, I've put you in an awkward position. It's just that the flowers…I thought they had come from you. So…Oh…I feel so silly now.' She shrugged off her embarrassment.

Marcus took a step forward and grabbed her hands. Christine couldn't meet his eyes. 'Christine. You are perfect, believe me you are…I mean this in a nice way, but even if you were the last woman on Earth…I wouldn't be attracted to you.' Christine flinched. Marcus's words cut deep. She wanted to run out of there and tried to pull her hands free, but he held on tight. 'Look at me, Christine!' She didn't want to. His voice softened.' Please look at me.' She lifted her head and looked into his eyes. His brow was furrowed and his eyes were sad as they appealed to her. 'Do you understand what I mean, Christine? Even if we were the last people alive, I *wouldn't* be able to be attracted to you, because I don't find *women* attractive.'

The penny finally dropped. 'Ohhh.'

'But please…keep that just between you and me.'

'I feel like such a fool, Marcus. I'm so sorry.'

'You have nothing to apologise for Christine. I wish I did fancy you. You are a babe.' The tension instantly vanished and Christine laughed. 'Come on, I owe you a drink in The Cheese Wedge and Pickles.'

'I'd say, more like two,' she joked. Marcus laughed and nodded his head. 'Okay, two it is. Let's lock up.'

Christine stood by the gate at the end of the small front garden and watched Marcus as he locked the front door. She hadn't seen *that* coming.

As they headed for the pub, Marcus crooked his arm and offered it to Christine. She curled her hand around it and they giggled together like a pair of young schoolgirls as they headed for the pub.

They stepped through the threshold of the pub still laughing, and that's when Christine's and Tom' eyes met. He slammed his pint of beer down on the bar and stormed out, pushing past Marcus.

Marcus leaned into Christine's ear. 'Now there's a man who would only want *you*. Even if he were the last man left on Earth and he had the choice of billions of other women.'

Christine's gut clenched into a tight knot.

Chapter sixteen

Christine woke up in a tangle of sheets. Her first thoughts weren't of work, they were of Tom. She'd felt awful all evening whilst she was with Marcus, being with him in body only, her mind elsewhere.

After a quick shower, she headed downstairs to make a cup of tea. She couldn't face breakfast—*she couldn't face Tom again*—but she had to. But what would she say? Her heart told her she wanted to experience more than friendship with him, but her head told her it was the wrong decision. She had other people to consider. She didn't want to upset Tom's daughters. That would doom their relationship from the start.

She paced in her small kitchen, sipping her tea as she contemplated what to do. Her first client wasn't booked in until eleven. Should she pay Francis a visit? Christine knew she worked from home. Before going through the pros and cons of such a visit, Christine grabbed her handbag and flew out of her front door before she changed her mind. Francis lived on the other side of the bay and Christine's nerves were frayed as she walked the narrow steep streets to get to her house.

The start of the day wasn't as sunny as it had been lately. In fact, it was overcast with light grey clouds, hinting at a spot of rain. Christine hoped it wasn't a macabre sign of the uninvited visit she was about to spring on Francis.

Pippa and Oliver were just leaving Oliver's family home with their pets, Ginger and Jess as Christine passed by. She lifted her hand in greeting. 'Morning. Looks like umbrellas

FINDING LOVE IN SEAGULL BAY

might be needed today,' she said as friendly as she could muster considering there was an orchestra playing in her head.

Pippa waved back. 'Morning Christine. I checked the forecast and there's a chance of rain in an hour, but it will be sunny the remainder of the day.' Christine smiled and nodded.

'Christine. As a regular at the pub, can I get your opinion on something?' asked Oliver, his American accent still strong after being back in the UK for months.

Christine stopped and turned to face him. 'Of course. What is it?'

'We have the chance of getting a county and western band to play at the pub this weekend. Do you think that style of music would be received well? Or should we look for an alternative?'

'Are they expensive?'

'Actually, they are free. This will be their first gig. They wanted a smaller audience to practise in front of. I know country music is popular in the states, but not so much here. That's why I have my reservations.'

'If it's free, it's a no brainer Oliver. Actually, I love country music. There's probably more people than you realise who like it in the UK, and the folk band went down really well at the summer bar-b-q.'

Pippa turned to look at Oliver. 'That's true. I noticed residents of all ages were up dancing to them.' She turned her attention to Christine. 'Thanks Christine. I think you're right. We should give them a try.' Christine smiled and nodded.

'Will we see you in there Christine now we know you are a fan of that music genre?' asked Oliver.

'You will. Have a great day.'

'You too, Christine,' said Pippa with a warm grin, waving as she turned around, Ginger pulling on his lead to start their walk. Oliver raised his hand in a farewell gesture as Jess led the way, slightly ahead of Ginger.

Christine sighed as she turned away and continued on to Francis's house. She really hoped she would.

Standing outside Francis's red door, her fist hovered inches from the door. She could hear Francesca playing just inside and the happy voice of the little girl was making her doubt her decision to visit. She couldn't bear the thought of upsetting things and not seeing the lovely little girl again. Children visiting the salon meant so much to her. She dropped her fist and turned around. But just as she was about to walk away, the door opened behind her.

'Oh Christine. You gave me a fright. I wasn't expecting anyone to be out here.'

Christine spun around to see Francis holding a black bin liner, almost bursting at the seams. She quickly walked over to the outside bin, opened the lid, and deposited it inside.

Francesca was standing on the threshold, pointing at her. 'It's the lady who made my hair sparkle again, mummy.'

Francis laughed softly. 'Yes, it is my angel.'

'I'm a fairy mummy,' said Francesca, crossing her arms in front of her chest, her face screwing up with annoyance.

Christine chuckled. 'Sorry. Did I start something annoying?'

Francis shook her head. 'No. Not at all. We love that she thinks she's magical.' She glanced back at Francesca. 'Go on in, before your fairy dust is blown away. I think this wind means we're expecting rain.' Francesca gasped and ran back into the house. Francis turned back to Christine with a slight frown, drawing her brows together. 'Is everything okay, Christine? I don't think I've ever had you call on me before.'

Christine's smile faltered. 'Erm. yes and no. But don't worry—it's nothing sinister. Can I come in?'

Francis's frown deepened, and she nodded and gestured for Christine to go on ahead. Christine stepped past the threshold into the hallway. She was immediately bowled over by the amount of family photos hung on the wall. Not only of Francis, Francesca and Ted, Francis's husband, but there were also lots of photos of Francis and Georgina as children with Tom. One immediately caught her eye. It was of a young Tom cradling a baby, sitting next to Francis' mother, Heather. Heather was looking at her husband and newborn baby with such love it made Christine's heart swell.

She heard the front door close and glanced at Francis who was looking to see which photo had caught Christine's attention. 'Ahhh. That's one of my favourites. I had it on my mantelpiece for ages, but I prefer it there now because I seem to be running up and down the stairs constantly with that little fairy in there, so now I get to see the photo at least twenty times a day.' Francis finished with a small laugh as she gazed lovingly at the framed photograph. She looked back at Christine. 'You know I've never even thought to ask. Did you know my mum well?'

Christine sighed with a thin smile as she shook her head. 'No sorry love, not well. I only knew her a little from one appointment she had with me just before she was due to give birth to your sister. It wasn't long after I first opened my salon. You see, I only moved here to the bay twenty-six years ago.

It was my husband who grew up in the bay. I came from the next town over. Although it never stopped me from coming into Seagull Bay, every chance I got.' Francis' face fell. Christine could see her disappointment. 'But you mum made a very big impression on me during that visit.'

Francis' face instantly brightened. 'Can you tell me anything you remember about her? Anything—even the most insignificant detail would mean a great deal to me.' She glanced towards the door to the sitting room where the sound of a children's TV program could be heard. 'Actually, do you mind if we go into the kitchen so I can keep an eye on the fairy? I don't want any mischievous fairy dust being sprinkled whilst I'm distracted.'

Christine smiled and nodded. 'Of course.'

Francis led the way, and Christine followed. The fairy was lying on her tummy in front of the TV with her chin resting on the heels of her hands and her legs pedalling backward and forwards intermittently. She giggled at something on the screen, totally oblivious to Christine and her mum walking behind her.

The small sitting room and kitchen was an open plan design, with the kitchen counter dividing the two spaces. Francis grabbed the kettle and took it over to the tap to fill. She looked at Christine as she turned on the tap. 'Tea or coffee?'

'Coffee please. Milk no sugar.'

Francis nodded and busied herself getting mugs and whatnot. She looked over her shoulder at Christine and looked pointedly at two bar stools. 'Sit down, Christine. Make yourself at home.'

The gesture eroded some of her pent-up nerves and she gladly took the weight off her not-so-stable legs. It was lovely having this special moment with Francis, talking about her mum, but the main reason for her visit was at the forefront of her mind.

Moments later, Francis set a mug down in front of her. 'There you go. Please continue, you were about to tell me about mum's visit to your salon.'

Christine nodded and waited for Francis to settle into the seat beside her. 'Yes. As I was saying, when she came for her appointment, she was pregnant with Georgina. She had this huge belly, which looked so out-of-place with her slender arms and legs. I really don't know how she managed.'

A faint smile dragged up the corners of Francis' mouth. 'I'm not surprised. Georgina was just over ten pounds when she was born, the little heffer,' she chuckled.

Christine smiled at Francis' comment.'I can remember her being so excited about the prospect of being a mum to two children, but I was surprised she didn't have a name chosen for the baby when I'd asked her. Then, you and your dad walked in. He was holding your hand. If I remember correctly, he'd had an emergency job or something and was dropping you off to your mum. You sat on your mum's knees, the only space you could fit on with her pregnant tummy, as I trimmed the back of her hair, and we continued our conversation about names. Out of the blue, you said you wanted a brother named George. Your mum had giggled and had said it might be a girl and you'd turned up your nose at the suggestion. She'd asked what name you'd choose if it was a girl.'

Francis was on the edge of her seat with wide eyes, transfixed by the conversation. 'And what did I say?'

Christine chuckled. 'You said, George again. Your mum laughed so hard, I'd had to stop cutting her hair. In the end, she suggested Georgina. You appeared to be happy by that and jumped down to run over to my magazine pile and flicked through them for the remainder of the appointment.'

Francis' mouth had dropped open. 'So I chose my sister's name?'

Christine smiled and nodded. 'It appears you did.'

She began to laugh. 'Wait until I tell her' Her eyes went wide again. 'Do you know how my name was chosen?'

Christine shook her head. 'I don't. You'll have to ask your dad about that.'

Francis was still smiling as she nodded. 'I will... Anyway, what is it that you wanted to see me about today?'

Christine took a sip of her coffee. Gulped, and inhaled deeply as she licked her surprisingly dry mouth considering she'd just drank. 'I don't know where to start, really.'

Francis's eyes were kind as she reached for Christine's forearm and squeezed it, before cupping her own hands around her coffee mug. 'Just say whatever comes into your mind and don't overthink it.'

Christine nodded. 'Your father and I have been friends for a very long time. But that's all it's ever been, a solid friendship and nothing more. But...' she hesitated.

Francis nodded. 'Go on,' she encouraged.

'But, these past few weeks, something has happened between us. There's been a shift in the dynamics of our relationship.'

FINDING LOVE IN SEAGULL BAY

There was a ghost of a smile on Francis' lips. 'Has dad asked you out?'

Christine shook her head. She didn't want to lie, but she needed to know how Francis felt about a possible relationship starting between herself and her father. She avoided answering. 'There's a mutual attraction between us.'

Francis nodded and the ghost of a smile broke into a huge one. 'That's fantastic. Dad has done nothing but talk about you for ages. I can't believe something hasn't already happened between you too, and why did he even bother dating that Jenny woman is beyond me when he's quite clearly had his sights set on you for as long as i can remember.'

Christine was dumbstruck. 'He has?'

'Yes. He's mentioned you on and off for years, and then when he got the contract with you to fit-out your new dog grooming room, he was like a giddy schoolboy. It was only then did it click that he'd been carrying a torch for you for a long time.'

Christine frowned. 'But he's been coming to me for advice about his relationship with Jenny.'

Francs shrugged. 'I don't know how middle-aged men's brains work, but they can't be much different to how the majority of men think. Maybe he was trying to push you into feeling something towards him by dating her, and then talking to you about her. Maybe trying to make you jealous or something?'

'So would you be okay with the idea of your father and I if we decided to date? Only, I don't want to spoil anything between us if it doesn't work out. I'd hate to think you might feel awkward and not want to come into the salon again.'

'Christine. I'm a grown woman, not a teenager. I've known you all my life. Our relationship would *never* become awkward.'

Christine reached across the table and placed her hand on Francis' arm. 'I really appreciate that, Francis. I adore you, Georgina and little Francesca. I've seen you both grow up.'

'Is this why you came? You wanted to see if I was okay if dad's and your relationship shifted from friendship to something deeper?'

Christine laughed softly. 'Yes, I suppose I did. However, I'm not so sure Georgina feels the same way?'

Francis frowned. 'Oh? What gives you that impression?'

'She came into the salon and more or less asked outright if there was anything going on between your father and me. Of course I denied it, because other than our attraction to each other, there isn't. She then told me in a round-about-way, she didn't want your dad getting hurt again.'

'I'm so sorry, Christine. I had no idea. She's always been so over-protective towards dad. She feels responsible for our mother's passing, but no matter how many times I tell, it wasn't her fault. Mom didn't know she had pre-eclampsia after her birth... Look, I'll have a word with her. She always listens to reason from me.' Christine smiled and nodded, but she wasn't so convinced. 'Besides, it will give me a chance to rub it in that I chose her name.'

Christine felt a tug at her skirt. She turned to see Francesca offering her a picture. 'Look. That's me with my wand. That's you, and I'm magicing you into my nanny.'

Francis gasped, her hands flying to her mouth. She looked at Christine. 'Oh my goodness, Christine. Is this a sign?'

Chapter seventeen

Christine felt like a cat on a hot tin roof waiting for her first client to arrive, but as she was standing in her usual spot by the salon window watching the people of Seagull Bay go about their business, she felt herself relax a little.

She played over the earlier conversation with Francis scene by scene. Had she jumped the gun by talking to Francis first before making amends with Tom after walking out on him when he'd asked her out on a date? There was no saying he still wanted to go on a date. No saying he still wanted to start a relationship with her. Or had it been the right thing to do, going to Francis first? At least she now knew if things didn't work out between Tom and herself, there would be no bad blood spilt between them. She chewed the inside of her lip. She just hoped Georgina felt the same way as Francis.

Anyway, that was by-the-by. The problem she faced now was, how could she make amends with Tom? What would she do now? Flirt with him each time she saw him? She shook her head and shivered. No, that was not who she was. Maybe *she* should ask him out on a date—as friends. She shook her head. No. That wasn't the way forward, either. That was still keeping him in the friend zone. She needed to be straight and broach the feeling she was getting for him.

And then, as if the princess fairy had magiced him there herself, there he was there.

Standing directly in front of her.

Their eyes locked.

He was looking in at her from outside the salon window.

Christine's heart leapt up into her throat. He was such a handsome man. Why hadn't she seen him in this new light years ago?

He pointed to the door and Christine nodded. They walked simultaneously over to it, their eyes not leaving each other. Christine's hand trembled slightly as she opened it.

'Morning Tom.'

'Morning Christine.' Her eyes fleeted across his face, searching for a sign—the sign he too was still interested in her—but his face was unreadable—emotionless. Her chest felt tight, her gut even tighter. 'I'm taking Rosie for a walk on the beach later. Around five. Do you fancy joining me? I-I need to talk to you. It's important.'

The spark that had been dancing in his eyes for weeks—years even—had extinguished. Christine felt numb. Had Tom been to visit Francis and she'd told him everything she'd told Christine? Was Tom embarrassed? Humiliated by his secret prolonged feelings for her? Had Tom already made up his mind that after finding this out and turning him down when he'd asked her out on a date, he in fact no longer wanted to pursue her anymore?

She nodded. 'Yes. I'll come straight from work. Shall I meet you at the bottom steps?'

He nodded and turned away without another word, striding away at speed. Christine watched his wide back and a knot of regret started to form inside her.

She closed the door and continued to watch him walk away. 'You are a fool, Christine.' She said aloud to herself.

A hand lowered onto her shoulder, making her jump. She swivelled on the spot to see Marcus gazing out of the window before looking down at her. 'There's still a chance.'

Christine shook her head. 'I didn't feel that spark coming from him this time, Marcus... I don't think he likes me anymore.' Christine could feel herself welling up.

Marcus shook his head. 'I can guarantee there is still an attraction there, Christine. Besides, contrary to belief, men can't just switch off their emotions as you females would like to believe.'

Marcus' comment brought a smile to Christine's mouth. 'Is that so?'

Marcus grinned with a nod. 'It is. And from now on, I'll let you into the secret mind of a man. Anything you want to know, just ask.'

'Thank you Marcus. I'm so glad you decided to rent my dog-grooming room.'

He pulled her in for a quick hug. 'And I'm glad you decided to rent it to me, otherwise I would never have met you and would never have contemplated working from a small seaside town, and I really love it here.' He held Christine at arms-length. 'Do you have any clients booked in from 4-o-clock?' Christine shook her head. 'Good. Keep that hour free. You can do your hair and I'll do your make-up.'

Christine's brow shot up. 'My make-up? What's wrong with my make-up?'

'Nothing. I love the way you do it—the natural look. But for this meeting, you need that little extra *je ne sais quoi*.'

'What?'

'Trust me. My big sister is a make-up artist. She grew experimenting and I grew up watching her. When I changed careers, it was a toss-up between dog grooming and studying to become a make-up artist and follow in the footsteps of my sister.'

'Well, I'm glad the dog grooming won, otherwise we'd have never met.'

Marcus nodded with a smile. 'Exactly. Just when you think things are going one way, fate steps in and intervenes and the man of your dreams asks to meet with you on the beach at five.'

Marcus winked and Christine smiled, hoping fate meant *the important thing* Tom wanted to talk with her about was *a good* something.

*

Christine stared at her reflection whilst Marcus hovered behind her. 'What do you think? It's just as subtle as how you apply your make-up, isn't it? But the moisturiser I used combined with the liquid highlight gives your skin a more youthful glow doesn't it?'

Christine fluttered her eyelashes and pouted her lips. She looked years younger. 'That's amazing Marcus. Do you use the moisturiser yourself?' He nodded. 'No wonder you look so youthful. I didn't think men used beauty products.'

Marcus laughed. 'Another misconception.'

She stood up and turned to face him. 'Do I look alright?'

'You look fantastic. You'll blow him away.'

Christine hugged Marcus. 'Thank you. I'll see you tomorrow.' Marcus headed for his dog grooming parlour and

Christine switched everything off, turned the sign to closed, and locked the salon door. With a small flutter in her tummy, she made her way to the seafront.

Usually, she'd take the time to check out her surroundings, but she was all coiled up with nerves she'd only ever experienced on dates, although her last date had been many, many years ago. But this was a meeting, not a date, she needed to remember that.

She still had her work clothes on. A light blue chequered long-sleeved shirt, rolled up to her elbows, and white trousers, thankfully still clean after a day of washing, cutting and styling other people's hair.

The seafront grew closer and the knot in her stomach pulled tighter. Then she spotted him and her breath caught in her throat. He was standing where he said he was going to be, but he'd changed out of his work clothes and was now dressed casually, in jeans and a shirt. Christine's chest fluttered.

She felt almost shy as she approached him. Rosie's tail wagged frantically the closer she got and before greeting Tom, she went down on her haunches to greet Rosie. 'Hello there you little sweet thing. Are you ready for your walk?'

Rosie yapped and tried to reach Christine's face to lick it, but Christine felt her bravado return and got back on her feet and straightened to look Tom in the eye. He squeezed out a smile and nodded his head in greeting. 'Glad you could make it.'

'I said I would.' The knot was back again, only this time, it was much tighter.

Tom gestured to the steps. 'Shall we go down onto the beach?'

Christine nodded and walked ahead, glad for the chance to be in front so she could take a moment to gather herself. She looked down the length of the beach to see how many holidaymakers were still there. There were a handful of couples, but the young families had already departed, gone off to feed their children.

They walked side-by-side in silence for the first few minutes, acclimatising to each other. The seagulls squawked, and the waves crashed, but neither of them spoke. Finally, Tom let Rosie off the leash and they stopped to watch her race back and forth chasing waves and then seagulls.

Tom suddenly grabbed Christine's shoulders and spun her around to face him. Christine's brow shot up surprised. 'I can't stand it any longer, Christine... I need to know. Are you and Marcus in a secret relationship?'

'What? Why would you think that?'

'You turned me down for a date...and before that, I saw you coming out of Katherine's house together, his arm around you. Are you planning on moving in together or something?'

Christine huffed a laugh. 'Don't be absurd. I was showing Marcus the house on behalf of Katherine.'

'Then...why did you dance with him and not me at the bar-b-q?'

Christine drew in a long breath and turned towards the sea again as she blew out she spoke from the heart. 'It was because I didn't want to upset Georgina.'

'Georgina? That makes no sense, Christine.'

Christine turned back to look at Tom. 'Tom, is it my imagination or have things between us changed? I've sensed a shift between us these past few weeks. I feel as though our friendship has changed into something more.'

Christine saw a flicker of emotion reignite in his eyes. 'Yes. Things have changed between us. That's why I asked you out on a date...which you ignored.'

'I'm sorry I did that, but I was confused and unsure of how the girls would react to us dating.'

'The girls? *My* girls?'

Christine nodded. ' I went to see Francis earlier today and she told me you'd been talking about me a lot recently. From hearing you talk about me, Georgina must have thought we'd already become more intimate, because before the bar-b-q, she came into my shop and asked if we were going to the bar-b-q together. I told her I was going with Morgan and you were coming with us, which was the truth. She appeared relieved it wasn't just the two of us and went on to tell me she didn't want you to get hurt again like Jenny had hurt you. I took that as a friendly warning to stay away from you. So when you asked me to dance and I saw Georgina looking our way, I declined. I love those girls, Tom. I've known them since they were young and I don't want to hurt them.'

Tom's brow furrowed. 'I'm confused. So, does this mean you feel the same for me as I do for you, but you won't take things any further between us for fear of hurting my daughter's feelings?' Christine raised her palms, getting ready to further explain, but Tom continued, not letting her speak. 'But what about my feelings, Christine?' he took a step closer, his eyes taking in every millimetre of her face. 'I've loved you from afar for years. I always looked for a signal if you felt the same way about me as I did for you, but there never was one. I was giving up hope and even reverted to online dating to see if meeting someone else would help me move on, but it didn't. It did however bring us closer together when you became my shoulder to cry on, and I revelled in the attention you gave me as we talked through that break-up. And then there it was. Just before Marcus showed up, you showed a spark of attraction towards me—the first time ever.' Christine's mouth dropped open. 'But with *him* also on the scene, I sensed hesitation. It's been driving me insane'.

Christine's pulse was racing, and her breathing had quickened. 'You've liked me for years?' Tom nodded. 'Didn't you realise you could have had any single woman living in the bay?'

'But I only ever wanted you, Christine.'

'Tom. I've been happy on my own since Sam and I divorced, until recently. Now all I want is you too—I'm ready to take our relationship to the next level.' He let out a gasp. 'But I'm scared, Tom. What if it doesn't work out between us? It will ruin our friendship.'

Tom reached out and stroked the side of her cheek. 'No, it won't. We'll always have a special bond. Just like the bond you have with my girls. Nothing will taint it. We've both suffered enough heartache. Now it's time to embrace heart-happiness.'

Christine giggled. 'Heart-happiness? Is that even a thing?'

He pulled her into his arms. 'It is now. It's *our* thing.' His face lowered to hers and their lips met for the first time in their decades old relationship, and to Christine's amazement, it didn't feel weird—it felt right.

Rosie's bark a little further along the beach than she should have been, pulled Tom's mouth away from hers. His twinkling eyes quickly took in every millimetre of her face and Christine sighed inwardly with happiness, her smile stretching from ear to ear when Tom grabbed her hand, entwining his fingers with hers, before pulling her in the direction of the bark.

Rosie had jumped into Ned's little boat, who was preparing to take it out to sea. He turned his head from side to side looking for Rosie's owner, and smiled when he saw them approach, his smile widening even further when he saw their hands entwined. 'I wondered who this little rag-a-muffin belonged to. Good job Laurel and Hardy aren't with me. They are a bit protective when it comes to old Bessie here.' He tapped the boat. 'Although I can't get them on her for love-nor-money.'

'Evening Ned,' said Christine.

'Sorry about that, Ned. Rosie's a rescue dog, but she seems to adore the water, so I'm guessing she must have lived close to the sea with her previous owner,' said Tom.

'She loves the sea, eh? Want to come for a quick sail around the bay?' He winked at them. 'It would make the perfect first date.' Tom and Christine looked at each other and laughed as they nodded simultaneously. 'Then climb aboard.'

Chapter eighteen

Tom stood on Christine's doorstep with a beaming smile. 'Ready?' He held his arm out and Christine took it.

He looked breathtakingly handsome in his chequered shirt, blue jeans teamed with a belt, cowboy boots and a stetson. 'I didn't know you owned a cowboy hat,' she smiled.

'There are a lot of things you don't know about me, my darling,' he replied in his best American drawl. Christine giggled.

They walked arm in arm towards The Cheese Wedge and Pickles and Christine felt as if she were walking on air. It was surreal. They had been friends for over two decades and an official couple for two days. Only Morgan, Ned, Brett, Marcus and Tom's girls knew about their relationship.

Her stomach pinched as she thought about what type of reception they'd get from Georgina when they entered The Cheese Wedge and Pickles and she was a bag of nerves as they walked into the bustling pub.

Friends and residents of the bay who they had both known for years shot glances in their direction and Christine was pleasantly surprised to see smiles curling on their lips when they saw Tom's arm wrapped protectively around her waist. They gave knowing nods as they realised they were an item.

A member of the band drew everyone's attention when he tapped the mic to see if it was turned on. He was dressed in similar clothes to Tom, but he was also wearing a denim jacket. 'Good evening. We are Sunset Cowboys. We want to thank Oliver and Pippa for giving us the opportunity to play our first gig here at The Cheese Wedge and Pickles tonight. I was asked earlier if we take requests. In answer to that, we have a set list we'll be playing tonight, but if we know the requested song, we'll be happy to slip in into our set for y'all.' He looked around at the other band members and they gave him a nod. He picked up a guitar and slid the strap over his head before returning back to the mic. 'Okay folks. There is plenty of room out here in front of the band, so I want to see y'all dancing.' He tapped his guitar, and on the fourth beat, the music began.

Tom leaned in close to Christine's ear. 'What do you want to drink, Christine?' The smell of Tom's cologne made her feel as giddy as a schoolgirl. 'Half a lager, please.'

He lifted his chin, gesturing towards a corner of the room. 'The girls are over there. They've kept two seats for us. Go on over and I'll get our drinks.'

Christine nodded and smiled, but her stomach clenched into a tight ball. She looked over to where Tom had gestured and saw Francis sitting next to her husband. There was no sign of little Francesca. Georgina was sitting opposite her, alone. Her attention was transfixed on the band.

Francis waved enthusiastically, her face beaming with a smile stretching from ear to ear. She was clearly pleased to see Christine and her father together. Christine smiled and waved back. Christine glanced at Georgina, but she was either ignoring her sister or she was genuinely engrossed in the band. Christine hoped it was the latter, but the knot in her tummy still tightened as she approached their table.

'Christine, you look fabulous. You and dad look like you've just stepped out of Nashville.'

Christine smiled at Francis and her husband. 'Thanks. We thought we'd make an extra effort to support the band. Where's Francesca?'

'We got a babysitter.' She glanced at her husband with a contented smile. 'This is our date night.' Christine nodded.

She turned to look at Georgina who was looking up at her, and she almost fell into a chair with relief when she saw a knowing smile on her lips. Georgina stood up and hugged Christine, bringing her mouth close to Christine's ear to speak over the music, which had suddenly increased a decibel or two. 'My suspicions were right, weren't they?'

Christine pulled away and grimaced. 'They were, but nothing had happened between us when you came to my salon. I hope this hasn't changed things between us.'

'Oh but it has.' Christine's chest tightened. Had she read Georgina's smile all wrong? 'It means I get to see you all the more and I don't have to use the excuse of getting my hair done to come and have a chat with you.' Christine gasped. Georgina's statement couldn't be more welcome. 'You've always been my favourite female friend of dads, and I'm glad it's you, and not one of them he's hooked up with.'

Christine laughed as relief washed over her. 'Hooked up with? Is that what they call it these days?'

Georgina joined in with her laughter. 'Yes, and there's plenty of other terms which no doubt you are going to hear as the news of your relationship spreads through Seagull Bay quicker than wildfire.'

They sat down and Christine leaned in to Georgina, scrunching up her nose as she spoke. 'So your dad has other female friends?'

'Believe me. You have no competition. Dad has talked about you for years. Only, it never clicked that he'd been carrying a torch for you until recently. He has eyes only for you.'

The band stopped and the pub's customers applauded. Tom appeared with their drinks and placed them down. He winked at his girls and they smiled up at their hero.

The singer's breathy voice came over the mike again. 'Thank you. We've already had our first request. This goes out to Christine.' Christine's eyes went wide as she looked up at Tom. He nodded, confirming the request had come from him. 'Tom wants you to know the lyrics of this song are exactly how he feels.'

Tom held his hand out, requesting a dance. Christine's heart pounded against her chest as heads turned their way. She took his hand and he pulled her to her feet, leading her onto the dance floor.

Tom held her closely in his arms as they danced and Christine rested her cheek against his wide chest. She spotted Marcus standing at the bar, smiling. He dipped his head just as the music began.

Christine inhaled Tom's cologne. She was in heaven as they swayed to the music and Tom sang word for word in husky velvet tones that wrapped around her heart, along with the singer.

Note to the reader, play *Forever and Ever* by *Randy Travis now!* Youtube link[1]

'You may think that I'm talkin' foolish.
You've heard that I'm wild and I'm free.
You may wonder how I can promise you now.

---

1. https://music.youtube.com/watch?v=gi6XwsR2hIY

This love that I feel for you always will be.
But you're not just time that I'm killin'.
I'm no longer one of those guys.
As sure as I live, this love that I give.
Is gonna be yours until the day that I die.
Oh, baby, I'm gonna love you forever.
Forever and ever, amen.
As long as old men sit and talk about the weather.
As long as old women sit and talk about old men.
If you wonder how long I'll be faithful.
I'll be happy to tell you again.
I'm gonna love you forever and ever.
Forever and ever, amen.
They say time takes its toll on a body.
Makes the young girls brown hair turn grey
But honey, I don't care, I ain't in love with your hair.
And if it all fell out, well, I'd love you, anyway.
They say time can play tricks on a memory.
Make people forget things they knew.
Well, it's easy to see, it's happenin' to me.
I've already forgotten every woman but you.
Oh, darlin', I'm gonna love you forever.
Forever and ever, amen.
As long as old men sit and talk about the weather.
As long as old women sit and talk about old men.
If you wonder how long I'll be faithful.
Well, just listen to how this song ends.
I'm gonna love you forever and ever.
Forever and ever, amen.
I'm gonna love you forever and ever.

Forever and ever, forever and ever.
Forever and ever, amen.'

The music stopped and rapturous applause erupted as people got to their feet.

Christine pulled away from Tom's chest to look up into his kind eyes. Tears had gathered on her lower lashes. 'How have I not *seen* you all these years?'

Tom smiled down at her. 'It doesn't matter. You see me now and you're mine forever and ever, and I'm never going to let you go.' he leaned down and kissed her.

'About time!' someone called out, and Christine could have sworn it was Marcus. Everyone in the pub burst out laughing and the band started their next song.

*

Tom had his arm around Christine's shoulders as they walked back home. Georgina and Francis linked arms and walked beside them. Francis' husband had gone ahead to pay the babysitter.

'Are you sleeping at our house tonight sis, so that the love birds can have a bit of privacy?' asked Francis.

'You don't have to Georgina. I don't want to feel as though you can't be at your own house if I ever stay over.'

'No, it's fine, Christine. I get to see my little fairy niece first thing in the morning when I'm woken up to toys being thrust in my face and a little voice saying, play with me, GG.'

Christine laughed. 'Is that her pet name for you?'

'Yup!' smiled Georgina with a smug grin, showing she secretly adored it.

Francis pulled her sister closer and squeezed her. 'Lovely name, isn't it, *Georgina*?'

'Yes sis, it's a lovely name. How many times am I going to have to hear you ask me that?'

Tom laughed. 'Do you want to know how we came up with your name, Francis?'

Georgina answered excitedly on behalf of her sister. 'Yes-yes. We do.'

Tom drew in a long breath to begin as they walked up the hilly road, taking them home. Christine turned her head from left to right, her heart swelling as she looked at the family she'd always wanted, who unbeknownst to her, had been just a stone's throw away her whole life. 'Well, it was mother's idea to name you after her favourite singer, Connie-...'

*

A Paul Watters recipe

Seafood Chowder
1 tbsp vegetable oil
1 tsp butter
4 potatoes(peeled and diced into chunks)
2 carrots(peeled and diced into chunks)
1 onion (peeled and chopped fine)
500mls (chicken stock) fish and chicken work excellent together
2 tbsp dried dill
200g seafood mix
2 salmon filets (cut into chunks)
2 smoked haddock filets (cut into chunks)
250mls cream
100ml milk
4 tbsp flat leaf parsley coarsely chopped

Let's get cooking everyone
Heat up the oil and butter in a saucepan. Pop in the onion, carrot, potato and dill. Stir continuously for about 5 mins. Pour over the stock, bring to a simmer, pop on the lid and cook for 15 mins.
Remove the lid, add in the fish, cream and milk. Allow to simmer (NOT BOIL) SIMMER for 5 /8 mins until the fish is cooked.
Add in the chopped parsley

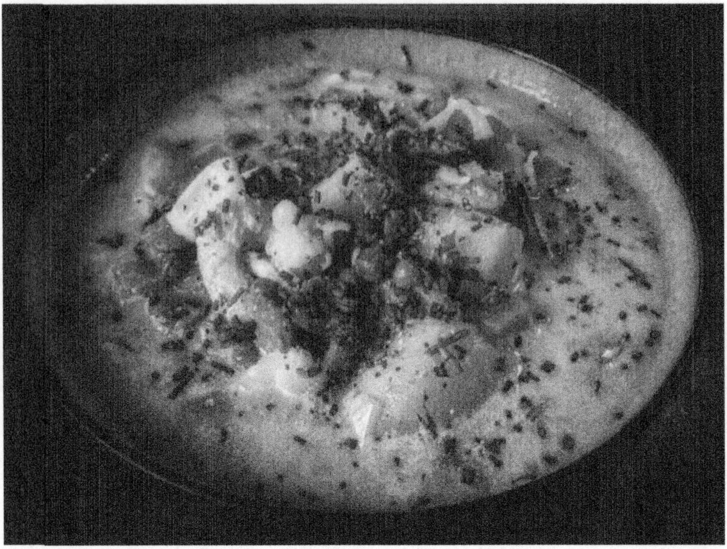

Next in Seagull Bay

[Pharis' Pickle in Seagull bay](https://www.amazon.co.uk/Pharis-Pickle-Seagull-Bay-heartwarming-ebook/dp/B0CJFWTDJY)

Printed in Great Britain
by Amazon